J.T. Edson
THE FORTUNE HUNTERS

BERKLEY BOOKS, NEW YORK

This Berkley book contains the complete
text of the original hardcover edition.
It has been completely reset in a typeface
designed for easy reading, and was printed
from new film.

THE FORTUNE HUNTERS

A Berkley Book / published by arrangement with
Transworld Publishers, Ltd.

PRINTING HISTORY
Corgi edition published 1969
Berkley edition / January 1983
Second printing / December 1984

ISBN: 0-425-07658-X

A BERKLEY BOOK ® TM 757,375
Berkley Books are published by The Berkley Publishing Group,
200 Madison Avenue, New York, New York 10016.
The name "BERKLEY" and the stylized "B" with design
are trademarks belonging to Berkley Publishing Corporation.
PRINTED IN THE UNITED STATES OF AMERICA

THE FORTUNE HUNTERS

CHAPTER ONE

The Deadest, Richest Man In Texas

The old man looked like a bag-line bum. He wore a cheap old woolsey hat perched on white hair that looked like it had been cut by standing a pie dish on his head and cropping around the bottom. The elements had given his face the texture and almost the color of old leather. A pair of gimlet-mean grey eyes peered suspiciously from under shaggy, beetling brows; a sharp nose seemed to be sniffing for trouble; and a mouth, thin-lipped and tight as the closed jaws of a bear-trap, made a slash over his sharp pointed, bristle-covered jaw.

Knotted around his throat hung a faded green bandana which trailed frayed ends down over a cheap washed-out blue hickory shirt. The black and white calfskin vest looked no newer than the shiny-seated black levis which ended thrust into a pair of ready-to-wear-boots; these latter a thing no cowhand worth his salt would be seen dead in. The gunbelt around his waist supported the weight of an old Whitneyville-Walker Colt; this at a time when the new metal cartridge weapon known as the Peacemaker had been on the market for long enough for most men to have put away their percussion-fired weapons and changed to the finest fighting handgun yet made.

Yet for all the poverty of his clothes, the old man rode a fine, spirited bay stallion. The saddle between his knees had seen many winters but bore the unmistakable

1

mark of a master craftsman's work.

Sitting slouched in his saddle, the old man watched a pair of cowhands engaged in their work. They were hazing along a bunch of cattle towards where the rest of the ranch crew held a branding herd. One of the animals, a big, mean black longhorn, burst from the bunch, taking off with the speed only his breed of the bovine world could work up.

One of the cowhands whirled his horse and took off after the fleeing longhorn. It had been giving much trouble and needed a sharp lesson, which same the cowhand intended to hand out.

His racing cow-horse closed on the fleeing steer and the cowhand leaned over from his saddle. Happen he made a slip, or his horse staggered, he would be unlikely to walk away from the fall. That did not deter him. Bringing his horse closer to the speeding longhorn, he stabbed out a hand to grab the animal'ș rear-poking tail. His hand closed on the tail and he jerked it towards him. Taken by surprise, and with it's balance thrown out of kilter, the steer's feet left the ground. It sailed over and crashed down hard enough to smash the breath from it. When the steer rose dazedly to its feet, it showed no inclination to head for the open range's freedom.

All in all the cowhand had given an inspiring display of part of his work, and performed a trick, upon the rough, uneven range country, that had dudes rearing up to applaud in excitement when they saw it done on the safe, even ground of a Billshow* performing ring.

The old man did not show any delight, nor even admiration for the cowhand's daring and his mount's skill and surefootedness.

"What in tarnation, thundering hell do you think you're doing?" he screeched, sending his horse down the slope towards the cowhand.

* Bill-show: A Wild West Show such as Buffalo Bill Cody toured the East presenting.

No cowhand was ever such a mild soul that he would have accepted that talk from a bag-line bum: one of the lowest of the low, a drifter who roamed the ranges begging food from cooks and avoid doing a lick of work in return. Yet the cowhand turned his horse towards the old man and answered in a reasonably civil tone.

"He's a bunch-quitter, Mr. Thackery. Figured to knock some sense into his fool head afore he got in among the main gather and started stirring them up."

The reason given for trailing down the steer was perfectly valid. It ought to have been completely acceptable to a man who knew cattle work and the peculiar mentality, or lack of it, shown by longhorn beef.

"Do you reckon I pay out thirty-five dollars a month for you to run the stock to hide'n' tallow?" the old man replied. "If you jaspers was worth your salt that steer wouldn't have had chance to jump the bunch. Damned if I know what the world's coming to. Time was a man could hire hands as'd do their work, without needing watching every damned minute of the day."

Swinging his horse, the old man rode off through the bushes on the slope. The cowhand watched him go, with an angry scowl on his face. Then he turned his horse and headed the subdued longhorn to the rest of the bunch.

"Who in hell does he think he is?" the cowhand growled to the other rider.

"Elmo Thackery, Tuck, that's who he reckons he is," grunted the other. "The richest man in Texas."

"Yeah? Well I'll tell you, Eddy, comes next payday I'm looking for a new boss. I rode for some mean cusses in my time, but he beats the living bejeesus out of them all."

"He don't pay good," Eddy, the elder man, admitted. "But the food comes up good, hot and regular."

"Which same's all that's kept me here this long," Tuck answered. "Only there's times when a full belly ain't enough."

They rode on, keeping the bunch of cattle moving

ahead and receiving no more trouble from the black steer. It appeared to have learned its lesson and would behave itself for the rest of the day. Keeping the bunch to the open bottom of the valley, the cowhands brought it around a corner and out into more open country.

"Hell fire, look there, Eddy!" Tuck snapped, stabbing out a finger.

A riderless horse came wending its way down the slope towards them. Some people might not have regarded the sight of a horse as being worthy of comment. As a cowhand who spent much of his life on the hurricane deck of a horse, the sight of another of the species *Equus Caballas Caballus* should not, and would not, have aroused any interest in Tuck's breast—except that the horse carried a saddle and no rider.

In the West a horse with an empty saddle always caused alarm. A man left afoot could only be in trouble and no time would be wasted in starting a search for him. This time the matter had added urgency for the horse was the bay Thackery rode when he came down to rebuke his rider.

Catching the bay, Tuck brought it back to where Eddy had already started to back track it. The two men rode through the bushes and up the slope from which the bay came.

"Know where we are, Tuck?" Eddy asked.

"Yeah. And I don't like it," the other man replied.

On reaching the top of the slope, the two men stopped their horses and peered ahead of them, scanning the bushes with intent gaze. Then they followed the tracks, noticing that the horse had been running.

"Up there!" Tuck growled.

"See it," Eddy answered, swinging from his saddle and leaving his horse standing with hanging reins.

Ahead of them the ground had been churned up even more than the running hooves of the bay previously marked it. Not only that, but a battered old woolsey hat lay by the marks and the bushes appeared to have been flattened over by some weight.

Moving forward on foot, the two cowhands cautiously advanced on the bushes and eased through. Their caution had good cause. Suddenly the ground just dropped away, falling over a hundred-foot into a sheer-sided ravine. The ravine had been masked from sight, even though about thirty yards wide at this point, by the bushes, a deadly trap for an unwary man. Its bottom lay covered in sharp spiked rocks, vicious looking points just begging for something to drop and be impaled on them.

Something had fallen and been impaled.

Something with shaggy white hair, a faded old bandana, black and white calf-skin vest, faded hickory shirt, both bulged up in an unnatural manner, shiny seated black levis tucked into scuffed-heeled ready-to-wear boots. A gun lay by the side of the still shape, having fallen from its holster.

"Whee dogie!" Tuck breathed. "We're looking at the deadest, richest man in Texas."

"Yeah!" Eddy replied. "Let's go back to the herd and fetch help."

"There's no rush. He must have landed on one of them spikey ole rocks, way his vest bulges up, and its gone through him like a butcher-bird skewering a bug on a thorn. We'll have one helluva chore getting him out of there."

"So Elmo Thackery's dead," Ole Devil Hardin said, looking at the man who stood before him in his gun-decorated study.

"Yes. I had a message telegraphed in this morning and came straight over to tell you the news."

The boss of the great OD Connected ranch sat straight-backed and stiff in the wheelchair which had been in his home since the day he tried, and failed, to ride the seventeen hand paint stallion his nephew and segundo, Rio Hondo gun wizard Dusty Fog, now used as his personal mount.*

For all that he was a few thousand dollars short of equaling Elmo Thackery's fortune, there was nothing of the shabbily dressed bag-line bum about Ole Devil Hardin. He wore an expensive broadcloth jacket, frilly fronted silk shirt and black string bow tie. From his waist down he was wrapped in a tartan blanket. His strong, aristocratic fighting man's face, with piercingly keen black eyes, showed no hint of self-pity or weakness due to his disability. Ole Devil was just as much the master of his ranch as he had ever had been.

"Why the rush, Gaunt?" he went on. "Pull up a chair."

Never had a man been so aptly named as the tall, spare visitor who stood before Ole Devil. With his black suit, white shirt and black cravat, and his lean gaunt face, the man might have been a successful undertaker in a wide-open trail-end town. Yet he was not. Ole Devil knew Frank Gaunt to be one of the shrewdest legal minds in Texas.

"Thanks, Devil," replied the lawyer taking a seat. "It's a strange thing, but Mr. Thackery had only been making arrangements to cover the event of his death just before I came down here. He might have anticipated it, for he had made full arrangements for the disposal of his fortune."

"Now me," Ole Devil interrupted dryly. "I'd have said if Elmo couldn't take it with him he wouldn't have gone."

A frosty smile creased the lawyer's usually sober features. Men who knew him claimed that Gaunt only smiled at real important folks who he admired and respected. He often smiled when talking to the boss of the OD Connected.

---

* Told in *The Fastest Gun in Texas* by J. T. Edson.

"I might have been inclined to agree with you," Gaunt replied. "Thackery had laid down certain terms, almost as if he expected to die during my business trip to Polveroso City."

"Huh?" grunted Ole Devil.

"He wants you to act as executor of his will."

"Me?"

"In a way. The will, as you might expect of Elmo Thackery, is an unusual document. I'm not even permitted to go into details of its contents as of yet. The one thing I can tell you is that Thackery left his entire fortune to be divided equally between his sister, Miss Mamie——"

"Good for Mamie," Ole Devil put in. "She stuck it out and lasted long enough to get something out of the old goat for all her years of hard work."

Ole Devil was no hypocrite and did not agree with the old saying about not saying ill of the dead. He knew Thackery too well to suffer from any illusions about the man and he had always admired Mamie Thackery for putting up with her brother's miserly, penny-pinching ways for so many years.

"Between his sister, Mamie," Gaunt continued. "His granddaughter Jennie. She lives at Casa Thackery and is the sole surviving issue of his second——"

"I know the family history," Ole Devil interrupted. "Elmo wanted to marry Jennie off to Dustine. How about his eldest boy, Pete, does he get anything?"

"He, or his surviving issue should he and his wife be dead, is included in the will on equal terms with the rest. So is Thackery's third son, Claude."

"I never took to Claude, too much like his old man," Ole Devil remarked. "He was the one Elmo sent to that fancy college back East, and who married that politician's daughter, the one the republican party threw out. Claude joined the same bunch. Took life real serious, did Claude."

"He took it so seriously that he had no children,"

Gaunt replied dryly. "He and his wife, Marlene, both get a share, so does Vint Borg."

"I heard old Vint died a couple of years back."

"He did. Lived long enough to see his son as Thackery's foreman in his place. So young Vint gets his cut. The other beneficiary is a woman, Joan Shandley."

"She's a new one on me," Ole Devil admitted.

"A saloongirl. It seems she met up with Thackery in Dodge at the end of a trail drive a couple of years or so back. Took him for a busted down old bag-line and staked him to a meal. So he's cutting her in."

"I'd never have thought of Elmo as being that kind-hearted," Ole Devil grunted. "Now what do you want of me?"

"For you to gather the various legatees and get them together at Casa Thackery to hear the will read."

"I'd be hard pushed to do that," Ole Devil replied, indicating the wheelchair.

"Your floating outfit could do it."

An explosive grunt left Ole Devil's lips at the suggestion.

"Do you think I can spare them to go roaming all over the West looking for Elmo Thackery's heirs?"

"That's one of the reasons I said it was almost as if Thackery had a premonition of death. Three months or so back he started the Pinkerton Agency searching for his heirs, the ones he couldn't locate personally. There were only the four who weren't at the house. Claude and his wife, Pete and, of course, the saloongirl."

"And Pinkertons found them all?"

"Sure. We know where to lay our hands on them at this time."

"Anyway, it's no use discussing the matter," Ole Devil drawled. "Dusty and the rest of the floating outfit are away on a trail drive. Fact being, they ought to be either very close to, or already arrived at Mulrooney by now."

For once in his life the lawyer showed his surprise. He

sat rigid in his chair and stared hard at Ole Devil for a long moment, then let out a long sigh.

"Lord!" Gaunt breathed. "It's enough to scare a man. Almost as if Thackery knew he was going to die and made all the arrangements for it."

"How do you mean?" asked Ole Devil, surprised at the emotion Gaunt showed.

"Pete is dead. Died last year. His only child, a daughter, Francine, wound up in the hands of a crook called Cohen in Chicago. The Pinkertons located her, but had been told not to make a move. The saloongirl is working in a place in Newton. Both of them within easy reach by rail from Mulrooney."

"And Claude and his wife?" Ole Devil put in, leaning forward and watching the lawyer's face.

"You know that Claude was active in Henry George's single tax doctrine movement? Well it has changed its name to the Socialist Labor movement now and Claude is one of its leading men."

"Which's just about what I'd expect of him," Ole Devil growled. "Where is he?"

"I'm not sure of his exact location. But Pinkertons found that he was starting on a political campaign, visiting the railroad towns to speak to the workers on their rights. According to the schedule Pinkertons supplied, Claude and his wife will be headed west along the railroad, making for the construction camps."

While not being a superstitious man, or one easily moved by coincidences, Ole Devil felt as if an icy hand had touched him. He shook off the feeling and turned his attention to the lawyer once more.

"Then they can all be picked up easy enough," Ole Devil said.

"Comparatively speaking. Pinkertons were asked to watch over them and report any change of location. It's uncanny how Thackery made his plans, almost as if he knew where the floating outfit would be. He sent the instructions to prominent lawyers in Dodge, Newton and

Mulrooney, to be handed over to his agents, with full
authority for them to make use of Pinkerton's services
in his name. So everything will be ready to show Captain Fog what to do and where he and his men must
go."

For a long moment Ole Devil sat in silence. A man
could trust Elmo Thackery to make some hawg-stupid
will and drop the handling of its provisions on
somebody else's shoulders.

However, Ole Devil owed Thackery a favor from
back in the old days before some twist of fate turned
Thackery into the scheming, suspicious, money-grab-
bing old miser he became. A man like Ole Devil Hardin
did not lightly toss aside his obligations. Under the circumstances there was only one thing he could say.

"All right. If you call out and tell them to rig my
buggy, we'll go into Polveroso City and send word to
Dustine."

"Certainly. By the way, Thackery authorized me to
pay you a bank draft for the sum of one thousand
dollars to cover the loss of time and expenses incurred
by the floating outfit——"

"Only he told you not to mention it until after I accepted, so that I wouldn't be tempted to take the chore
for the money," grinned Ole Devil. "That's typical of
Elmo Thackery. He lived mean and he died the same
way."

CHAPTER TWO

Captain Fog Meets Mr. Cohen

The Right Honorable Lady Winifred Amelia Besgrave-Woodstole—or as she was better known, Freddie Woods, co-owner of the Fair Lady Saloon and mayor of Mulrooney, Kansas—sat on the edge of her bed and rolled a black silk stocking up over her very shapely leg.

Thinking of the previous night, Freddie smiled. If anybody would have told her a man would attract her in such a manner, she would have laughed in the teller's face. Several men had tried; rich men prepared to drop their all in her lap; handsome men with a string of female conquests behind them. Until last night all had failed to attract the beautiful and mysterious lady mayor of Mulrooney.

True, the successful man had made quite a name for himself. He had been a Confederate Army captain at seventeen, with a name as high as Turner Ashby or John Singleton Mosby's ever stood. With the war over, he did not sink into oblivion and dreams of past glories, but had become the segundo of the OD Connected ranch and famous for his ability both as ranch foreman and trail boss. It was he who tamed a tough Montana mining town when three good, but lesser, men died trying.* And he became Mulrooney's first town marshal, responsible for framing the laws which made Freddie's

* Told in *Quiet Town* by J. T. Edson.

city into the one Kansas trail drive end where a Texas man received a fair deal. Folks claimed he was the fastest gun in the West, and Freddie did not dispute the claim. Nor was he a mean hand with bare fists in a roughhouse brawl.

A man with such a reputation and capabilities should, by popular conception be a veritable giant, handsome as a god of old and fully able to attract the favors even of as discerning a lady as Freddie Woods.

Dusty Fog stood five foot five and a half inches in his bare feet. Although she had long since forgotten the point, Freddie was a good two inches taller than him. His dusty blond hair looked tousled as he stood washing the shaving-lather from his face in Freddie's small bathroom. While he was good looking, he did not have eye-catchingly handsome features, yet there was strength in his face if one took time out to look. He seemed more impressive with his shirt off, for then the spread of his shoulders, the powerful muscles, lean waist and generally strong physique showed their full potential. One was inclined to pass Dusty by and ignore him as a small, insignificant cowhand when dressed, for he did not have the flair to best set off his expensive clothes. His black Stetson hat, with a Texas style low crown and wide brim, hung on the chair where rested his gunbelt, a matched brace of bone handled Colt Civilian Peacemakers, butt forward for crossdraw in the holsters. His new bandana and shirt lay among Freddie's clothes, his boots and socks with Freddie's shoes and a pair of button tipped rapiers on the floor.

He had just completed a trail drive and last night had been one to howl.

In many ways the trail drive had been a swine. Dusty brought it north earlier than usual and they hit swimming water over the willows in three rivers, but forced their way across. The bad luck dogged them and was only averted by damned hard work on the part of every

man of the trail drive crew. A bunch of rustlers tried to
hit the herd six days from Mulrooney, only to be driven
off and trailed to their hide-out. The rustlers had been
busy, with a herd of five hundred head of unbranded
stock to show for their efforts. After the shooting ended
Dusty took the cattle as compensation for his trouble.
He still brought in the first drive of the season and sold
it for top prices. Then, as he promised he would, Dusty
threw a party for his men in the Fair Lady Saloon.

Just how he and Freddie ended up in her private suite
of rooms, Freddie could not remember. They left while
the party was at its height; with Freddie wishing her
partner, Buffalo Kate, had not gone East on vacation,
for this celebration would be Kate's idea of fun. In the
suite Freddie and Dusty shared a bottle of champagne.
Then she insisted he ran a few passes with the dueling
swords, for Freddie was an unconventional young
woman and could handle a blade, saying it was good
exercise for her figure. After that things took their
course and Freddie had no cause for complaint.

A knock sounded on the door, it opened and
Freddie's maid entered with a buff colored telegraph
form in her hand. Crossing the room, she handed the
form to Freddie without even a glance at the open
bathroom door.

"It's for you Dusty," Freddie called.

Dusty came from the bathroom wiping his face with a
fancy, soft white towel. He stopped dead as he saw the
maid, but her back was to him and she ignored his
presence. Crossing to where Freddie sat, Dusty took the
paper and read its message.

"What is it?" Freddie asked.

"Darned if I know," he replied. "It's from Uncle
Devil, says for me to go see Counselor Talbot as soon as
I can and tell him I'm Elmo's Thackery's agent, then do
what he wants doing."

"Talbot?" Freddie asked in a puzzled voice. "He's

my lawyer. But he won't be at his desk until after nine o'clock. Will this work he has mean you'll be leaving Mulrooney immediately?"

"I don't know. It most likely will though."

"Oh!" Freddie sounded disappointed.

"I'd best get the boys woke, in case it's urgent," Dusty drawled.

"Martha will do it for you," Freddie answered, watching him start to don his shirt. "It seems a pity to waste time until nine o'clock though."

"Sure," Dusty smiled, watching the maid leave the room.

Freddie removed the stocking she had put on and yawned, stretching. "I think I'll be lazy and have breakfast in bed," she said. "Did you ever have breakfast in bed, Dusty?"

"Only when I was sick."

"You're looking a little peaked right now," Freddie said, and Dusty took off his shirt again.

On leaving the bedroom in which he spent the night, Mark Counter walked to the next door and pounded on it.

There stood a man who might have served as a model for what Dusty Fog should look like by popular conception. Six foot three inches in height, with a costly white Stetson hat on his curly golden blond hair. He had an almost classically handsome face, yet one with strength of character and intelligence. Great wide shoulders tapered down to a slim waist, clad in an expensive tan made-to-measure shirt over which the ends of a scarlet-silk, tight-rolled, bandana hung from his throat. He wore levis which had been made for him, for he would have had difficulty to obtain such a perfect fit by buying off a storekeeper's shelves. His high-heeled, fancy stitched boots had been made by the same master hand which tooled his gunbelt. The matched ivory butted

Colt Cavalry Peacemakers hung in contoured holsters built for speed on the draw.

He was Dusty Fog's right bower, and a man in his own right. During the war, Mark rode as a lieutenant in Bushrod Sheldon's cavalry regiment. He gained a name as a brave fighter, and the Beau Brummel who set uniform design fashions among the bloods of the Confederacy. Now his taste in clothes dictated rangeland fashions among the Texas cowhands. His strength was a legend, his prowess in a roughhouse brawl spoken of with awe wherever it had been witnessed. Few could say how good he might be with his guns. The few who *knew* claimed Mark to be second only to Dusty Fog in the matter of speedy withdrawal and accurate shooting.

The door swung open under Mark's push and he found his good friend, the Ysabel Kid locked in the arms of a very pretty red-haired girl.

Clad all in black, from hat to boots, the Kid stood six foot, with a lean, wiry, whipcord strong frame. His hat hung on his back by its storm-strap and his hair was curly, black as a raven's wing. Looking at the Kid's tanned face, one might put his age at a young sixteen, so almost babyishly innocent were the features. Then one saw the eyes, they did not look sixteen years old, but cold, red-hazel, savage and ancient in wisdom.

There was something wild, alien about the Kid, Indian-like almost. His father had been a wild Irish-Kentuckian, his mother of mixed Comanche-French Creole blood. From these parents he gained a sighting eye like an ancient mountain man and an almost uncanny skill with a rifle. He could handle the ivory hilted bowie knife which hung at the left side of his gunbelt with the skill of old Jim Bowie himself and might be accounted fair with the Colt Dragoon revolver pointing its walnut grips forward in the holster at his right. Fair in Western terms meant he could draw in around a second and hit his man at the end of that time. He spoke several

Indian tongues and fluent Spanish, could track where a buck Apache might fail, slide through thick bush with the silence of a shadow.

Taken any way one looked at it, the Ysabel Kid made a good friend, or a real bad mean enemy.

"What the——?" he began, turning towards the door.

"Dusty wants us downstairs *pronto*," Mark replied.

Holding the girl at arms' length, the Kid looked down at her. "*Adios*, honey lamb, happen we have to pull out."

"I hope you don't, Loncey," she replied, using the Kid's Christian name.

Turning, the Kid walked from the room, passing Mark and not noticing his big *amigo* had not followed him. Mark stepped forward, scooped the girl into his arms and gave her a kiss. Her arms closed around him, gripping him tightly and she looked a trifle glassy-eyed when he released her.

"Are you going too?" she asked.

"Why sure," he grinned, "We'll maybe see you around."

"I'll be here," she breathed.

Mark left the slightly dazed looking girl and found the fourth member of the floating outfit already in the hall.

His only name was Waco. A tall youngster in his late teens, he came between Mark and the Kid in height, though showing a developing muscular heft to his wide shoulders and lean waist. He had curly blond hair, a tanned, handsome young face with blue eyes and a mouth which now smiled easily. From his hat to his boots he spelled tophand Texas cowboy, his clothes modeled on Mark's design. The gunbelt supported a matched brace of walnut handled Army Colts. Waco had ordered a brace of the new Peacemakers, but they had not yet reached him so he retained his old armament. From the way the belt and guns hung, he did not wear them as decorations.

"Sleep well, boy?" asked the Kid, although he looked younger than Waco.

"Why not?" Waco replied with a grin. "I got me a clear conscience."

There had been a time when Waco's conscience might not have been so clear. Left an orphan almost from birth, the youngster had been raised on a Texas ranch. At thirteen he never moved without an old Navy Colt thrust into his waistband. By the time he reached fourteen, Waco had killed his first man, a bunkhouse bully of the worst kind. Two years later Waco rode for Clay Allison's CA outfit, and no man, or boy, worked for that Washita curly-wolf unless he could handle his guns. Waco had been well on the trail ridden by Wes Hardin, Bad Bill Longley and many another handy Texas boy, with a quick gun and a foot on the slide. Then he met up with Dusty Fog, Mark Counter and the Ysabel Kid. After Dusty saved his life, Waco followed the Rio Hondo gun wizard with almost dog-like devotion and hero-worship. Now Waco rode as a member of the elite of the OD Connected crew, Ole Devil's floating outfit. From the other three, who treated him as a younger brother, he learned much and was now regarded as a respectable and very useful member of rangeland society.

The three cowhands went downstairs and sat at a table, to be served by a couple of Freddie's girls with heaped-up breakfast plates. They all settled in to eat with good appetite, but their leader did not make an appearance through the meal.

"I wonder what Dusty got us down here for?" Mark asked, glancing at Waco who sat wolfing his food down. "Boy, you're eating like it's going out of style."

"Young feller like me needs his victuals to keep his strength up," Waco replied, swallowing a mouthful of ham and eggs.

Not until almost nine o'clock, when the three cowhands were muttering dire threats against him for dragging them away from their business without good cause, did Dusty join them downstairs. He crossed the room and sat at their table, meeting their gaze without any hint of shame for keeping them waiting.

"What kept you-all, Cap'n Fog, sir?" asked Waco, who had risen and politely drawn a chair out for Dusty to use.

"I've been using a boss' prerogative, boy," Dusty replied. "Having breakfast in bed. Say, that food smells good. Go raise me a plateful, will you, Waco?"

From the hearty meal Dusty ate, the other three concluded the food upstairs had not been as plentiful as served out to the peasants down below.

"What now, Dusty?" asked Mark. "And if it's word from Ole Devil, don't tell us, let us suffer."

"Sure," the Kid agreed. "Why I near on asked that lil gal to marry me.—Say, Ole Devil wants us to do something urgent, don't he?"

"We have to see a lawyer," Dusty replied, not failing to notice the hopeful note towards the end of the Kid's words. "After that, *quien sabe*?"

"I don't and that's for sure," groaned Waco. "But I'll just bet my tired lil Texas bones it means work for us."

They found out what was needed of them soon enough. Talbot had been notified of Thackery's death and already consulted the Pinkerton field officers to learn of the location of the missing heirs to the fortune. This pleased Dusty, for few Texans wished to have anything to do with the Pinkerton Detective Agency. When Dusty left the lawyer's office he knew what he had to do, and where to find the people he wanted.

"We'll have to split up," he said as they sat in the Fair Lady saloon following the visit to the lawyer's office. "I'll telegraph Ed Ballinger and ask him if he can meet up with me. He'll likely be able to find this Cohen feller. Mark, you take the train up to the construction camps and pick up Claude Thackery and his wife."

"How about the hosses, Dusty?" asked the Kid.

That would be a problem. None of their personal mounts took kindly to strangers handling them, and the Kid's huge white stallion could be dangerous even with people it knew. They could not leave the horses in a livery barn, nor with the OD Connected's remuda, for that would be headed back home in a couple of days along with the chuck and bed wagons.

"You and the boy take my paint and Mark's blood-bay with you," Dusty replied, after thinking the matter over. "Go by hoss and across country to Newton to meet up with the Chicago at around noon tomorrow."

"How about you, Dusty?" Mark asked.

"I'll take the noon train east. It's a fast mail and I'll be in Chicago at around noon tomorrow. Happen I'm lucky, allowing for a day to find the girl, I'll be back here on Friday. It'll take you about that long, Mark."

"Sure," Mark agreed.

"And us, if we go on hoss back," the Kid drawled. "Huh! Apart from taking me away from the gal I love, this'll be an easy enough chore. Once we've got them to Casa Thackery, we'll have finished with it."

Which only went to prove that although the Ysabel Kid might be a damned efficient scout, a fighting man from soda to hock, and no mean hand at wooing a pretty little gal, he made a damned poor prophet.

Chicago had already proceeded well on the way of removing the traces of its great fire of 1871. The main railroad depot could equal anything the eastern cities had to offer, both in grandeur and amenities.

While not being a naïve country-boy getting his first sight of a big city, Dusty still felt relieved to see the big, craggy shape of Detective Lieutenant Ed Ballinger coming through the crowd of people: passengers from the fast mail train, people coming to meet friends or relatives, railroad officials and just folk who had nothing more important to do than come and see what the trains brought in.

"Howdy, Dusty," Ballinger greeted, holding out a powerful hand. "Good to see you again."

"And you," Dusty replied, giving as good as he got in the firm handshake.

"Come on. I've a hack waiting to take us to the Stockman's Hotel. I booked you in there. My place is being painted out and I'm living, if you could call it that, at the headquarters station house."

They made a contrasting pair as they walked side by side from the railroad depot and on to a busy street. The big city detective in his curly brimmed derby hat, grey suit of the latest eastern cut, white shirt and stiff collar and the black tie; and the small Texan in range clothes, with a buckskin coat, and carrying a warbag in his right hand.

"What's your interest in Abe Cohen?" Ballinger asked as they sat in the carriage on their way to the hotel.

"He's got a kid——"

"He's got a dozen or more of 'em. Hires them out as shoeshine boys, flower girls, things like that. They pick pockets and steal anything that's not nailed down. Only we can't bring it back to Cohen. All he does is hires the kids out to work, which's fairly honest."

"Where do we find him?" Dusty inquired.

"In the Bad-lands. I'll take you after we've fed and got you settled in," Ballinger replied. "How's Mark, Lon, Waco and all the folks back to Rio Hondo?"

"Fit as fleas and twice as lively," grinned Dusty.

"Mark wanted to come with me, but I said you'd most likely got enough vices without him introducing you to any more."

An answering grin creased Ballinger's rugged face. There had been a time when he regarded all westerners as dull-witted yokels fit only to be rooked by quick-thinking city slickers. Then he went to Texas after a gang of Chicago crooks and his path crossed that of the Rio Hondo County bunch. During a hectic month-long visit, Ballinger saw much to change his opinion of westerners in general and this small, soft-spoken insignificant Texan in particular.

"It's a pity Mark didn't come," Ballinger remarked. "In more ways than one. That's a mean area we're going into."

"I'm dressed," Dusty replied quietly.

Looking down, Ballinger could see no sign of Dusty's gunbelt and Colts. Yet he knew the range term Dusty used did not mean that he was wearing all his clothes.

"You'd best remember the Chief of Police don't go for gun fight around his town," Ballinger warned. "We're civilized here—or so they tell me."

The Stockman's Hotel was one of the better places in the stockyards area of town and catered for visiting ranchers, cattle buyers and other people with an interest in Texas' main industry. Consequently the desk clerk had some knowledge of famous Western names. So he did not conceal his surprise too well when a small, insignificant cowhand announced himself to be Captain Dusty Fog. However, the clerk knew Ballinger and so did not argue. Giving Dusty a room key, the clerk called a bell hop forward to carry the warbag and show Dusty to his room.

"That's one of the new model Colts, isn't it?" Ballinger asked as he sat on the edge of the bed and watched Dusty remove his jacket.

"Sure. Civilian Model, four and three-quarter inch

barrel. I bought a brace just over a year back, when they first came on the market. They're the guns I used down in Mexico.''*

While Dusty washed and shaved, Ballinger examined the bone handled Colt the small Texan had carried in his waistband. Although the detective felt curious about Dusty's interest in Abe Cohen, he asked no questions, for he knew Dusty would explain everything in his own time.

After a meal in the hotel's dining-room, during which Dusty explained the reason for his visit, the two men left the building. Hailing a passing carriage, Ballinger told its driver where they wanted to go.

"That's a bad neighborhood," the driver objected.

"So they tell me," Ballinger replied, taking out the wallet which contained his detective lieutenant's badge, and showing it to the man. "Does that make you feel any better?"

"Naw!" grunted the man. "But I'll take you."

"You can stop out front of Henderson's if you like," Ballinger growled. "We'll go the rest of the way on foot."

The driver looked slightly relieved at the suggestion.

"That'll be all right," he said. "I never heard of anybody getting robbed or killed in front of Henderson's—in plain daylight."

"I thought you said this's a nice, quiet, civilized little town," Dusty remarked to Ballinger as he climbed into the carriage.

"Sure it is. Why up in Streeterville you'd think you was in fashionable New York, it's that genteel—trouble is we're not headed for Streeterville."

Passing the stockyards, the carriage took its passengers through the sprawling area known as the Badlands. Here the great fire had wreaked its most terrible havoc, already new houses had been built. The new

---

* Told in *The Peacemakers* by J. T. Edson.

houses, even so soon, were fast taking on the look and smells of the old slums which the fire removed.

Ragged children stopped their playing to stare at the carriage as it went by, keeping a watchful eye on the driver's whip. Dirty, untidy men and women stood silently scowling at it, wondering who might be inside. Four big, burly policemen, patrolling in the smallest safe number for that area, gave the carriage a hard, watchful, suspicious study. No honest man in the Bad-lands could afford to ride around in a carriage and visiting dudes meant trouble for the patrolmen when they visited the saloons and drinking houses of the area.

At last the carriage came to a halt on a street which appeared to be lined with saloons, gin-palaces and other places of entertainment, so in consequence looked in far better condition than most of the surrounding district.

"Stay here and wait for us," Ballinger told the driver as he sprang from the carriage.

"H—here?" gulped the man, throwing a nervous look around.

"That's what I said. We'll not be more than fifteen minutes."

"B—but——!"

"Just a minute," Ballinger grinned, knowing the cause of the man's worry. He crossed the sidewalk to the doors of the big, garish looking saloon and yelled, "Henderson!"

A burly, red faced man wearing a loud check suit and a revolting clash of color in vest, shirt and neckwear, came to the saloon's door. His surly face twisted into what charitably might have been described as a welcoming smile as he looked at Ballinger.

"Yerse, Mr. Ballinger?" he said in a grating Cockney accent. "What can I do fer yer?"

"I'm leaving this feller out here. See he's kept safe."

"That I will. He'll be as safe as if he was me own."

The driver looked much relieved as his two passengers

walked along the street away from him. In the Bad-
lands, Henderson's name carried much weight and no
man under his protection need be afraid—at least not in
plain daylight and before Henderson's front door.

"Where now?" Dusty asked as they walked along the
street.

"Down here," Ballinger replied, swinging into a
narrow street with rows of three-storey houses flanking
it. "This's the one here. Cohen own the place, lives up
on the top floor. If we're real lucky we'll get up there
before anybody recognizes me and warns him."

Inside the building a foul stench hit Dusty's nostrils,
the smell of unwashed bodies, urine and excreta, the
aroma of a slum.

"Lord!" he said. "What a way to live."

"Yeah," Ballinger replied. "And Cohen's probably
got more money than a lot of folks living in big man-
sions up in Streeterville. Let's go."

They went up the stairs which felt slick and greasy
with filth underfoot. Just as they reached the second
floor, a small, rat-faced man stepped from a room. He
stared at Ballinger, his mouth dropped open in surprise,
and he turned to dash towards the stairs leading up to
the third story.

Springing forward Ballinger shot out his left hand to
catch the man by the collar and haul him backwards.
The detective's other hand went into his jacket pocket
and came out with a short, leather-wrapped, lead-
loaded, police billie. Even as the man tried to yell a
warning, Ballinger's right hand lifted and he brought
the billie down. He struck only once, with the skill of
long practice, and the crook collapsed in a limp heap to
the floor.

"Let's move!" Ballinger snapped, bounding over the
man's still body and heading upstairs with Dusty on his
heels.

On reaching the third floor, which was no cleaner
than the rest of the house, Ballinger led the way towards

a door. From behind it came a flat "splat" and a high
pitched scream, the cry of a child, or girl, in pain.

"We'll have to bust it in!" Ballinger growled. "It'd
take more than one man though."

"What're we waiting for?" Dusty answered.

Abe Cohen was handing out a disciplinary lesson to
one of his workers. Always a man who demanded
results, he did not take kindly to failure, especially
repeated failure. With his door locked, he thought
himself safe from interference, so gripped the pretty, if
dirty, black haired girl by the arm with one hand, the
other lashing his thick belt across the back he had exposed by ripping open her flimsy ragged dress. Half-a-
dozen other ragged boys and girls in the middle teens
stood around the room, flattened back against the walls
and watching the thrashing in silence.

"I'll teach you to come back empty handed!" he
bellowed, swinging up the belt again.

Then the door burst open. The door he had prided
himself on as being strong enough to prevent such
unauthorized entry. Swinging around, Cohen opened
his mouth to snarl out something. Releasing the girl's
wrist, he let her fall in a sobbing heap on the floor.

On bursting into the room, Dusty and Ballinger took
in the scene before them. Ballinger felt rage welling up
in him. Yet he was bound by certain rules, for there
were defenders of the right of the people who would be
only too willing to jump on him should he hand Cohen
the thrashing the man so richly deserved.

Dusty had been a lawman, but held no official post in
Chicago. For all he cared, the defenders of the rights of
the people could go climb their thumbs. He saw
something which made his temper rise, and he was just
the man to do something about correcting matters.

"You lousy, stinking skunk!"

The words left Dusty's mouth as he shot forward. His
right fist drove out, the knuckles exploding on Cohen's
mouth, snapping the man's head back and staggering

him away from the girl. She crawled weakly across the room. Vicious weals left by the belt showed across her back. Glancing at the girl, Dusty saw the marks which proved to be unfortunate—for Cohen.

"Why, you short runt!" Cohen gasped, spitting blood. "I'll tear you apart."

"Keep out of it, Ed!" Dusty barked.

Leaping forward, Cohen lashed his hand around. The belt coiled up and behind Cohen then slashed forward across Dusty's back. The small Texan felt the bite through his jacket, shirt and undershirt, so could guess how the girl must have suffered. Even as Cohen drew back his hand for another blow, Dusty sprang in. Two punches then a knee smashed into the bigger man's stomach. Cohen gave a squawk and staggered back, his hands dropping to his sides. Jumping forward, Dusty stamped on the belt buckle and pinned it to the floor. He ripped a punch to Cohen's jaw and sent the man backwards, causing him to lose his hold on the belt. Cohen swung a blow which caught Dusty at the side of his head and knocked the small Texan staggering.

Stabbing down his right hand, Cohen brought a knife from his pocket, jerking open the blade. He had everything in his favor, or so it seemed, height, weight, heavy muscles and a knowledge of roughhouse fighting, yet he still pulled the knife.

"Leave him!" Dusty roared at Ballinger before the detective could move.

Snarling like an animal, Cohen came forward. The knife licked out towards Dusty's body in a vicious upwards slash.

"Yeeah!" Dusty yelled, jerking off his hat and throwing the heavy Stetson full into Cohen's snarling face.

His sudden move distracted Cohen and in almost the same movement Dusty showed some of the Oriental fighting science called Karate which he had learned from Ole Devil Hardin's Japanese servant.

Leaning his body to one side, Dusty raised a leg and swung it in a circular motion so that the edge of his foot smashed against Cohen's knife-wrist. The blow came so unexpectedly, and with such power, that Cohen thought his wrist was broken. The knife clattered to the floor and Cohen twisted desperately away from Dusty. Twice more, almost too fast to follow, Dusty kicked, smashing the ball of his foot into Cohen's side. He sent the burly man reeling across the room and caused some of the watching youngsters to jump hurriedly aside.

Cohen felt as if his ribs had been caved in. The *keriwaza* kicking techniques of karate were very effective and deadly when performed by a master like Dusty. In fact Dusty refrained from using his full strength when delivering the kicks for he had no wish to kill the man.

Once again Cohen flung himself into the attack, relying on his extra weight to smash Dusty down; which was a hawg-stupid way to go about handling Dusty Fog if Cohen had but known. Dusty did not try to avoid the rush. Instead he moved to meet it, left hand catching Cohen's right arm just behind the elbow, left foot moving into place to allow him to pivot so his hips rammed into the other man. At the same moment Dusty brought his right arm twisting around and under Cohen's trapped limb and gripping his own left wrist for added leverage. Bending his legs and inclining his body forward, Dusty catapulted Cohen straight over his shoulder.

To the watchers it seemed that Cohen had taken wings, for the man sailed up in the air and landed with a crash on the table in the center of the room. It crumpled under the man's weight, legs collapsing and drawer bursting open. On the whole, even though a Colt Cloverleaf revolver lay inside, Cohen would have preferred the drawer to stay closed while Detective Lieutenant Ballinger was present. Inside the drawer lay a pile of wallets, watches, purses and other items gathered in by his youthful employees during their morning's work.

Ballinger saw the contents of the drawer and sprang across the room to slam the door and lean his back against it to prevent a mass departure by the youngsters. Seeing that they were trapped, the youngsters settled back to watch their employer get something they had hoped he would receive.

Knowing that Ballinger had spotted the loot, Cohen rolled onto his stomach and grabbed for the gun. Dusty sprang forward fast. It was no time to think of fair fighting, for he was not sure how efficient Cohen might be with a revolver.

Down smashed Dusty's right boot heel, grinding on to the back of Cohen's hand and crushing it on the hard butt of the Cloverleaf. Cohen screeched in pain, his fingers opening and his torso rearing upwards in agony. Round lashed Dusty's left foot, exploding under the man's jaw and almost lifting him erect. Limp as an unstuffed rag-doll, Cohen collapsed to the floor.

Dusty might have left it at that, but he chanced to see the girl crouching against the wall and sobbing, the welts of the belt showing on her bare shoulder. Bending, Dusty grabbed Cohen by the back of his dirty vest. With a heave, Dusty fetched the man upwards, almost ripping the vest and shirt from his back and bringing him to his feet. Dusty released his hold and threw his right fist with all his strength behind it. Fist met jaw with a click like two enormous billiard balls colliding. The blow brought a wince of sympathy from Ballinger. It shot Cohen across the room to land him in a limp heap beside the girl he had been beating.

Mutters of delight and amazement came from the youngsters as they stared bug-eyed first at Cohen's sprawled out body, then to where Dusty picked up his hat and set it at the correct "jackdeuce" angle over his off-eye.

"Which of you's Francine Thackery?" he asked.

"She is, mister," one of the boys replied, pointing to the girl Cohen had been flogging.

A frightened, dirty and tear-stained face lifted to Dusty's as the girl huddled back against the wall.

"What do you want with me, mister?" she asked. "I never stole anything. That's why he was thrashing me."

"Easy now," Dusty answered gently, holding out his hand to her. "You're coming out of here with me."

"Wh—where to?"

"Your grandfather's ranch in Texas."

"It's a lie!" the girl gasped. "My grandfather wouldn't lift a hand to help me. Pappy always said he was the meanest man alive."

"He's dead."

Gently taking the girl's arm, Dusty helped her to her feet. At his touch the girl's fear died down and hope took its place. Only for a moment did the hope remain, then it died off again. She knew much about the evil power of the man on the floor. His house was filled with men who dare not allow him to be arrested for he swore he would turn State's evidence on them if the law should ever take him.

"Cohen's men will never let you through," she warned.

Pushing himself away from the door, Ballinger walked across to the room window and tried to raise the sash. It would not budge, so he wasted no more time. Picking up one of the chairs, he smashed it into the window, shattering the glass and sash. Then he took out a police whistle and began to blow it lustily. Other whistles sounded and Ballinger knew he would soon have help on hand.

Seeing their chance, the youngsters all dashed for the door tearing it open and fleeing. The sound of their departure brought men from other rooms, standing in the corridor until the shrilling of the police whistle brought their attention to Cohen's room.

"Stop the kids, Dusty!" Ballinger yelled, hearing them making for the door.

"Let 'em go. You've got that feller with all the evidence against him," Dusty replied. "You keep blowing that whistle——"

His words ended as the first of the men came into sight, crowding towards the door of the room. They were big, surly, evil looking men wearing town clothes of various standards of value, and came with knives or clubs in their hands.

"Keep back!" Dusty snapped.

The men fell back, those in the lead hurriedly reversing direction. It was partly the magnetism of Dusty's personality, and partly the bone-handled Colt in his right hand which stopped the men. For the most part these town toughs tended to be knife or club wielders and only used guns as a last resort. So they had never seen a real frontier trained gun-fighting man in action and did not know just how fast and deadly one could be.

To the men it seemed that the gun just appeared in Dusty's hand. Only he did not look small to them. In some way he seemed to have put on size and bulk until he made the tallest among them feel small.

Ballinger also held a gun, a short Webley Bulldog revolver with a kick like a mule and plenty of power. Yet, in some mysterious manner, he did not give out the same menace as exuded from the small Texan.

"Right back, keep moving out!" Dusty ordered, moving forward.

Before his advance the toughs fell back, across the corridor until they hit the other wall.

"You'll not get out of here alive, cowboy!" yelled a man from the safety of the crowd's rear.

"Then six of you'll go with me," Dusty answered calmly. "Who's first taker, gents?"

Watching Dusty, Ballinger could not help but admire

his quiet courage and dynamic personality. All too well
the big detective knew he would have failed to cow and
drive back that hard-case bunch with a gun in his hand.
Yet Dusty did it.

"Who's up there?" roared a robust Irish voice.
" 'Tis the law asking."

"You boys had best head for the hills," Dusty said,
gesturing with his gun. "There's no way you can stop us
now."

"He's right!" a man yelled. "It's every man for himself!"

Dropping his club, the man turned and dashed along
the corridor towards the end window. Panic was always
infectious. Clubs and knives rained down as the other
men scattered in their mad haste to escape before the
law fell on them.

Heavy feet thumped on the stairs and a quartet of
brawny policemen reached the third floor with their
clubs in their hands. They came cautiously, for four
would not be a large number to take on the gang Cohen
kept around to protect his interests.

"What the devil?" asked the leading man, staring
to where a couple of crooks struggled to crawl from
the corridor window.

"Let 'em go, Reagan," Ballinger said, stepping
from Cohen's room. "We'll gather them in later.
Come in here, I've a present for you."

"Holy mother of God!" the policeman gasped as
he entered Cohen's room. "Did yez do that to him,
Lootenant?"

"No, Cap'n Fog did. Let's get help here. We've got
Mr. Cohen where we want him and we're going to
take this joint apart. There'll be a lot of folks buying
trunks before we've done here today."

The burly policeman stood and stared at Ballinger.
Clearly he did not understand the old western term
Ballinger used. Out west when a new and efficient
lawman came to a town, a number of undesirable

people who had been residents for some time could be seen buying trunks ready to pack their belongings and leave. So the term came to be used when undesirables had to leave town in a hurry, whether they bought trunks to do so or not.

Apart from not understanding the term, the policeman eyed Dusty with frank disbelief. It did not seem likely such a small man could have felled Cohen single-handed.

Dusty did not bother to try to convince the policeman, having enough on his hands explaining to a very frightened Francine that her troubles were over and, after he had her cleaned up and fed, he would take her to Texas far beyond the reach of Cohen and his kind.

"Come on, honey," he said. "I'll take you out of here."

"But what about Cohen's men?" she gasped. "They might be waiting on the street."

"Likely they'll let us by."

Although Dusty spoke in a quite, gentle tone, there was nothing gentle in his eyes. Remembering how Cohen's men, who she thought to be so tough, had backed away before the small Texan's menace, Frankie knew he spoke the truth.

Four more policemen arrived and Ballinger told off two of them to go with Dusty to Henderson's place.

"There's a hack stood outside. Go with Cap'n Fog in it. He'll drop you off at your station house. Let him go on to the Stockman's Hotel, and you tell your captain to load every paddywagon with every man he can spare and send them down here as fast as they can."

The two policemen thought they were being sent to guard the small cowhand and the girl, keep them safe through the danger area. It would have surprised them to know Ballinger was sending them along with Dusty so that he could protect them.

On leaving the building, the two policemen exchanged

glances as they saw the sullen-faced crowd across the street. Taking a firmer grip on their night-sticks, they started forward.

"Keep close to us, mister," the bigger policeman said.

Neither attached any significance to the way Dusty changed the scared little girl from his left to his right arm holding her arm firmly yet gently; nor in the way Dusty opened the front of his coat. All the policemen knew was that the crowd had not made a single move to stop them.

"That's him!" a man, who had climbed down a drain-pipe and crossed from Cohen's told the people around him. "He may look small, but he's got two sawed-off shotguns under his coat and he can get them out quicker than you can blink an eye. And don't laugh. Bully Claggert's headed for the railroad depot he's so scared."

"Keep clear of them while they've got that cowboy with them!" another man told those closest to him, having made good his escape from Cohen's. "That's Wild Bill Hickok, the famous western killer. He's got two revolvers under his coat and the way he looked when he pulled them on us, he was just hoping for a chance to throw lead."

Dusty would not have been pleased to know who the man claimed him to be.

"They've got Cohen," yet a third deserter from the house across the street informed his cronies. "I'm pulling out while I can."

Like flames leaping across dried grass, the words passed among the crowd. Fear of the consequences of Cohen's arrest filled everybody with anything dishonest on their consciences—almost every member of the crowd in fact—and sent them scurrying to their homes to gather portable belongings and make hurried departures for other hide-outs.

"I can't believe I'm free and won't never have to go back there again," Francine breathed as she sat in the coach with Dusty.

They had dropped the policemen off and were now on their way to the Stockman's Hotel.

"How'd he get hold of you in the first place?" Dusty asked.

"Pappy owed him some money. So he said I should get work to help pay it off. Cohen sent me out as a flower girl. It wasn't until Pappy died last month that Cohen started to tell me to steal. He taught me to pick pockets and said I had to bring home something each day if I wanted to eat."

"And did you?"

"Y—yes—— When I was hungry. I might have tried to run away, but one of the other girls tried. They caught her, some of Cohen's men, and brought her back. Cohen made the rest of us watch what happened to her. I wake up at nights screaming when I dream about what they did to her. And I didn't dare escape."

"It's over now," Dusty told her quietly. "Cohen's going to jail, and if I know the sort of folks he works with, they'll tell the police everything when they get caught. Your troubles are over, Francine. Or will be when I get you to Texas."

CHAPTER THREE

Miss Shandley Meets Two Texas Gentlemen

"Where at'd a feller find Joan Shandley, friend?" the
Ysabel Kid asked.

Looking towards the speaker, the bartender of the
Buffalo Hide Saloon made a mistake. Before coming to
Newton the bartender had worked in a Dodge City
saloon much patronized by the Earp brothers. Except
when absent on business trips—the trips always coin-
ciding with the arrival of some Texas trail crew headed
by a man noted for his speed and skill with his
guns—the Earps kept cowhands firmly in their place
and the bartender tended to look down on them. He expected cowhands to speak deferentially to him.

"Over there, playing poker," he grunted and started
to turn away.

"Which one'd she'd be?" Waco inquired.

Swinging, the bartender looked the two cowhands
over, seeing two young men who, at first glance, seemed
to be no different from a hundred or more who visited
Newton every trail season.

"Why?" he growled.

"She's my mother," Waco answered.

"Yeah," drawled the Kid, "and I'm related to him on
my father's side."

Something in each young man's appearance and attitude warned the bartender not to push things too far.
Under the bar lay a twin barrelled ten gauge, its barrels

cut short to spread the shot better when fired. Glancing
at the two tall young Texans, the bartender decided they
would be ten gauge meat—happen a man had the guts to
reach down and lift it. Only the man had best be able to
lift the shotgun in less than a second, or he would likely
die trying.

There was another point to remember. This was
Newton, not Dodge City and he did not have the Earps
to back him—always assuming the Earps would chance
tangling with those two Texan boys.

"No offence, gents," he said. "Only Joan
don't——"

"Who said we wanted to?" growled the Kid. "You
likely wouldn't believe us, but we done come to tell her
she's inherited a fortune."

The bartender felt undecided. Maybe that black-
dressed heller with the Comanche-mean face had made
a joke and expected laughter to applaud it. Or again
perhaps he did not want a laugh. Either way, the wrong
response could be equally fatal.

"That's her, the brown-haired little gal in the blue
dress, just dealing," the bartender said in a more civil
voice. "Can I get you anything?"

"Two schooners of beer," Waco drawled. "And take
something for yourself."

Deciding the two Texans were maybe nicer gents then
he first imagined, the bartender collected the drinks.
Then he leaned an elbow on the polished bar top and
jerked a thumb in the direction of the table across the
room where a poker game attracted a lot of interest and
attention.

The poker game attracted attention for two reasons:
first, the players were saloongirls; second, they were not
playing for money.

Nobody could ever say Homer Trent failed to provide
his customers with entertainment. He had needed an attraction to counter the crowd-drawing show at a rival

establishment and, as the new town marshal of Newton allowed a certain freedom to such places which crossed his palm with silver, organized a poker game between five of his most willing and attractive girls.

While the idea proved to be a success and pulled a good crowd into the Buffalo Hide, Trent could not honestly claim to have been the first to use it. He had heard of the owner of another saloon using the same method to counter the drawing power of a rival's show.

Anticipation ran through the crowd as the small, pretty, brown-haired woman in the blue dress dealt the cards. Most of the jewelry had been bet and this deal ought to prove interesting.

"I'll open," Beegee Benson said, taking off her wide-brimmed flower decorated hat.

Joan Shandley and Beegee Benson might have been sisters, so alike were they in height and build. The only difference noticeable at a distance was that Beegee wore a flame red dress of daring cut and had piled up blonde hair. For the rest, they had good figures; pretty, but not ravingly beautiful faces; and neither would see thirty again.

The betting went briskly, for the girls wanted to get the game over and resume their normal work. Only Beegee and Joan seemed to take it seriously, for they alone had insisted that whatever they won from each other would be kept as in a real game.

At last only three players remained. Joan, Beegee and a young redhead. Having been told by their boss how far they could go, Beegee and the redhead called Joan's bet while still wearing their brief underclothes, although they had bet jewelry, hats, dresses, slips, shoes and stockings; removing them and putting them on the table used for the pot.

"I'll see it, three fives," the red head stated.

Joan smiled. "I knew I had you beat, Red," she said. "But I was scared that Beegee might fill her straight."

"And I did," Beegee whooped delightedly, turning over her cards. "Five to nine, climbing up. Read them and weep."

"Oh, I beat that too," Joan put in as Beegee's hands went towards the pot. "Three threes and two kings, full house. Hard luck, darling, anyway you ran a good second."

For a moment Beegee sat eyeing Joan, a flush climbing up her cheeks. Joan tensed herself ready for an attack. It would not be the first time she and Beegee had tangled.

Two things stopped Beegee from jumping Joan; they were not dressed for a brawl; and the boss had given them definite orders. Not that Homer Trent had any scruples or dainty feelings to cause his objection to the girls fighting. He remembered the time he brought together a pair of lady gamblers in a saloon he owned down Texas way. Trent had not needed two gamblers, but hoped to gain some publicity by a fight between them. He succeeded, partially, in his wish. The girls put on a fight, but unfortunately it spread to the crowd and before Trent could stop it, his place had been wrecked.*

So Homer Trent fought shy of such lusty entertainment as arranging, or allowing, spontaneous brawls between his female employees.

Draping a cloak around her, which gave her some slight coverage in excess of her underwear, Joan scooped up what money had been used in the game. The other girls knew their property would be returned in the back room and so did not raise any objections as Joan yelled that she would buy drinks for the house. Beegee was the exception to the rule. Due to her boasting before the game, Beegee and Joan had insisted they would play for keeps.

"Get your drink, boys!" Joan called. "And you, girls. Then I'll go put on my new hat and frock and

* Told in *The Wildcats* by J. T. Edson.

come back to let you see how it looks.''

Picking up the red dress and Beegee's hat, Joan nodded to the waiters, who carried the rest of the pot into the back room to be collected by its owners. Joan headed for the bar, receiving congratulations and compliments from all sides.

"Excuse me, ma'am," a soft drawling voice said behind her.

Turning, Joan looked at the two tall young Texas men who stood side by side and clear of the crowd. She studied their trail stained clothes and their weapons with some interest. A woman did not work in saloons all her grown life without gaining a knowledge of men. Joan reckoned she could read the signs pretty well. Two cowhands, young men, yet handy and capable. They did not appear to be drunk, nor had they the look of a pair of men who wanted female company.

"Everybody was included when I shouted for the house, boys," she said. "So belly up and call your poison.''

"We were hoping you'd join us at a table, happen you're Miss Joan Shandley, ma'am," the Ysabel Kid replied.

"My, aren't you the choosey one?" she smiled.

"There's an empty table across there, ma'am," Waco drawled. "We'd like to talk to you.''

"Go ahead.''

"Away from the crowd," the Kid suggested.

Once more Joan studied the lean, Indian-dark faced boy—or was he a boy? Her second look led her to believe that black-dressed Texan was older than she had first imagined.

"These boys wanting something, Joan?" asked a bouncer, moving forward.

Some instinct told Joan the two Texans meant her no harm; anyway she reckoned she could handle any cowhand in her own country. Another instinct warned her that it might go badly for the bouncer, despite his superior size and heft, if he tangled with that salty looking brace of Texans.

"It's all right, Benny," she said, then smiled at the Texans. "Come on, boys. Do you want a drink?"

"No, ma'am," Waco smiled. "But you might."

"Might I?"

"Sure, ma'am. Set, me 'n' Lon here, well we know what we're going to tell you and you don't."

Joan signaled to the nearest waiter and told him to bring a bottle of whisky and three glasses to her at a table. Then she led the Texans clear of the crowd and sat down with them. Already Trent had his show starting on the stage so as to hold on to the customers who came in to see the poker game.

"Do you know why I've come with you?" she asked, determined to get things straight from the start.

"You're curious," Waco suggested.

"And you're too smooth for your age," she answered, hoping to cut him down to size and show him that she was used to older, mature *men*. "I came to see if you *boys* had a new line. Most of you, depending on how long you've been chasing the Swamp Lightning, want to know what a nice gal like me's doing in a place like this and can you marry me and take me away from it all."

"Well, we did kind of figger on taking you away from this, all right," the Kid admitted.

"And marry me?" she smiled. "Both of you?"

"Always did want to marry rich," Waco drawled. "But I reckon you'd be too smart to take me."

"Well, that needn't worry you. I'm not rich. How about your friend?"

"Me, ma'am?" grinned the Kid. "I wouldn't marry anybody who'd marry a mean ornery cuss like me. We'd still like to take you out of here and make you rich."

The smile left Joan's face and it set in hard, warning lines. Yet she could not decide what to make of the two cowhands.

"I don't know where you boys heard about me, or what you heard," she said grimly. "But you heard wrong."

"You're not Joan Shandley, ma'am?" asked Waco.

"Sure I am. But I don't——"

"I wouldn't spit in their faces if their mouths were on fire," interrupted the Kid, "but I'll say one thing, Pinkertons aren't often wrong."

"How'd you like to be rich, ma'am?" Waco went on.

"I reckon I'd best get Benny over here."

"You got a grudge against him or something?" drawled the Kid. "Or maybe you just don't like the idea of being rich."

Joan had started to rise, meaning to yell for the bouncers and to hell with the consquences. Then she sat down again and looked at the two young men. If they were wanting to sleep with her for the night, they sure showed a strange way to go about it. Most men tried to act as if they were doing her a favor and that she ought to be paying them. Not that Joan made a habit of entertaining the customers that way, but a saloongirl often received offers.

"Did you ever see a drama, ma'am, where the heroine buys some old down-and-out drifter a meal, only he comes out to be real rich and leaves her all his money in his will."

"Sure, I've played the heroine," she replied. "Corn like that goes down well with the rubes."

"Reckon that play Lon talked about couldn't come true then?" Waco grinned.

"I only wish it would for me."

Reaching out a hand, Waco took the whisky bottle and poured out a stiff drink, pushing the glass towards Joan. Then he nodded to the Kid.

"There's seven of you to share it," drawled the Kid, never taking his eyes from Joan's face. "But I'd say your cut'd be nearer two hundred thousand dollars than one."

"What's this all about?" Joan asked, searching their faces for some hint of cowhand humor and finding none.

"Do you remember back when you was working in the Bon Ton in Dodge, and you set an old feller up with a meal?" asked the Kid.

Screwing her face in a puzzled frown, Joan thought back to all the times she had bought needy folks meals. At first she could not think of any old man while she worked for the Bon Ton, in fact she had not been long in the Bon Ton's employment, having a rooted objection to sleeping with the customers, picking pockets and rolling drunks even if the place did have the patronage and support of the Earp brothers.

"Sure!" she said, slapping her brow. "Some old bag-line bum——"

"His name was Elmo Thackery," the Kid put in.

"Oh sure," Joan answered. "And you're Dusty Fog."

"No, ma'am. I'm some better looking than Dusty. 'Sides which he's gone to Chicago after Thackery's niece. I'm the Ysabel Kid and this's Waco."

"You're serious!" she gasped.

"No, ma'am. The Ysabel Kid, like I told you. And Elmo Thackery's done left you a share of his fortune. All you have to do is go to Casa Thackery with us and see a lawyer."

"Nice feller, Elmo Thackery," Waco carried on after the Kid stopped speaking. "Or so somebody said, least-ways, somebody somewhere must have said so."

Joan barely heard a word Waco said. She turned a dazed, unbelieving face to the Kid and asked, "You mean that old feller I bought a meal for was Elmo Thackery, the richest man in Texas?"

"Why sure, though I wouldn't say he was the richest. I ride for Ole Devil Hardin myself."

Ignoring the cowhand belief that his boss must be the best man alive, no matter what aspect was being discussed, Joan shook her head as if to clear it.

"And he's left me some money?" she gulped.

"We don't know how much," Waco replied, grinning. "But he left you an equal share with six other folks. Reckon you could use that drink now."

"I reckon I could," Joan agreed and sank four fingers of rye whisky in a single gulp.

The bite of the raw liquor ragged her and made her cough, bringing tears to her eyes. However it also served to force coherent thought into her head. Such things did not happen in real life, folks didn't come into a saloon and tell you that you'd come into a fortune—only this pair of cowhands had just done so.

"If this's a joke!" she warned grimly.

Taking a letter from his pocket, the Kid slid it across the table to Joan. She took it up, extracted a sheet of paper from the envelope and read its contents with growing amazement and certainty that this was *not* a joke. Or, if joke it be, those two Texans had gone to a lot of trouble and expense to put it over on her.

"I can hardly believe it," she said. "You know what I'm going to do?"

"No, ma'am," grinned the Kid.

It was on the tip of Joan's tongue to say she aimed to treat the house to decent drinks instead of the cheap whisky which had been served the first time.

"How soon can you start back to Mulrooney with us, ma'am?" Waco asked before she could speak.

"Mulrooney? I thought the ranch was in Texas."

"Sure it is," agreed the Kid. "But we're meeting some of the other folks, who get a cut of the will, down there."

"I'll catch the noon train tomorrow. But this's my night to howl."

Grins came to two Texan faces. Way they saw it, Joan had a right to howl and they reckoned they could help her do it.

"How do I attract folks' attention?" Joan asked.

"You want to?" grinned the Kid.

"Sure."

Rearing up from his chair, the Kid threw back his head and let out the most hideous scream Joan had ever heard come from a human throat. Waco added a wild cowhand yell and Joan, though taken by surprise, came in with a screech like a train going through a tunnel.

On the stage a group of tumblers had reached the high spot of their act and all six of them stood in a human pyramid. The yells spoiled their concentration and the pyramid collapsed faster than it had been built. Every eye turned to Joan and her companions, the floor manager started forward with a couple of bouncers tagging along on his heels.

"Yahoo!" Joan yelled. "Hit that bar again, boys, and serve them some decent liquor for once, you bardogs! Take the show folks a bottle of champagne."

"Have you gone crazy, Joan?" the floor manager growled.

"I've just had good news," she replied.

"You're stunk-up drunk!" the manager spat out and eyed the two Texans. "And you pair best look through the doors."

"Hold it, Stan!" Joan snapped.

Stan held it. He noticed that the bouncers showed a marked reluctance to tangle with the two young cowhands. Also he felt curious as to why Joan, who he knew could hold her liquor, should act in such a manner on the few drinks she had taken that evening.

"What's it all about?" he growled.

"The lady's done come into money, friend," the Kid drawled.

"Look at this, Stan," Joan went on, handing the man the letter.

Although he considered himself a shrewd poker player, with a face that gave only such indication of his emotions as he wished it to, Stan stared bug-eyed at the paper after reading a couple of lines. The more so because he had worked in Mulrooney and recognized Lawyer Talbot's handwriting. Here was no cowhand joke, Joan really did have a share in a sizeable fortune.

"Well," Joan said with a smile. "Do I set them up?"

"Sure you can," the floor manager replied. "Good for you, Joan."

By now the crowd realized something of more than usual importance had happened. Western crowds were never noted for looking gift-horses in the mouth, especially when the gift-horse carried free drinks with it. Once more they swarmed to the bar to accept Joan's hospitality, although on this occasion they were treated to much better liquor, for the bartenders read the floor manager's sign correctly.

"Hey, Red," Joan said, catching the arm of the girl who shared the last pot in the card game. "Where's Beegee?"

Of all the people in the saloon good old Beegee must be the one to help Joan celebrate. Joan intended to return all Beegee's belongings, including the fancy red dress Beegee sneaked out of a shop knowing Joan wanted it. Not that Joan objected, given half a chance she would have done the same to Beegee. They had been friends for more years than either liked to think about and Joan wanted Beegee to share her good fortune. Perhaps Beegee would come along with her to collect the money, then settle down in some permanent town and open a dress shop. It had been their ambition to do so, even though neither of them really expected to ever achieve it; and both were reaching the age where the better class saloons thought twice before hiring them.

"She went out, looked all riled up," Red replied, pulling her arm free so as to head for the bar and collect her free drink.

Wasn't that just like old Beegee though? Getting her wild up and storming off when Joan had good news to share with her. All right, if that was how she wanted it, that was the way Joan intended to play it.

For the first time Joan remembered how little clothing she wore. A grin came to her face. She reckoned Beegee would be fit to be tied if the blonde saw her in the red dress and wide brimmed hat. When Beegee got that way, things were likely to pop and Joan was so happy she wanted to do something violent. To hell with Homer Trent's orders, after tonight Joan and Beegee would not need to care what the saloon's owner thought.

"Look, boys," she said to the Kid and Waco. "I'm going out the back and to the hotel to dress and fix my face. Come on down in about ten minutes and meet me. We'll hooraw the town."

"Whatever you say, ma'am," the Kid replied.

"Hey, Joan!" yelled a woman. "You're not running out on us now you're rich, are you?"

"Nope!" Joan yelled back and the crowd fell silent to hear what she had to say. "I'm just going to the hotel to change into Beegee's frock and hat, then I'm going to howl."

Picking up the red dress and hat, Joan entered the back room to gather up the jewelry which lay scattered on the table after the other players in the game had helped themselves to their property. It would make old Beegee pot-boiling mad if Joan turned up wearing her jewelry as well as the dress and hat.

Joan left the saloon by the rear door and went along the back alley to the small flea-bag hotel where she roomed. Nobody was in the hall and Joan climbed the stairs to the poorly lit passage where her room lay. She unlocked the door, pushed it open and entered.

A noose of rope dropped over her head and shoulders and clamped tight on her arms. The hat and frock fell from her hand, she let out a startled squeal and felt herself being pushed forward towards the bed. Two more loops of the rope came over her head and drew tight on her arms. Taken by surprise, Joan could not stop herself being shoved forward until she fell face down on the bed. A knee rammed into her back, holding her down, a mouthful of bed clothes prevented her from screaming; not that it would have done much good screaming, for the hotel catered for saloon workers, most of whom would be out at work.

Struggling wildly, but with no result, Joan felt her hands drawn behind her back and secured. Her unseen attacker sat with knees astride her and weight on her back. Then the weight eased off, a hand gripped her hair, pulled her head up from the pillow and, as she opened her mouth to scream, released the hair and pulled one of her own stockings around her face in a gag.

Rolling over, Joan found herself looking up at laughing Beegee. Bending, Beegee grabbed one of Joan's ankles, reaching for the other leg. Kicking wildly, Joan tried to buck herself free of the hands which held her ankle and escape from the ropes. Twice Beegee grabbed and missed, then managed to get a noose around the free ankle and draw the rope tight. She ignored Joan's angry splutters as she fastened the ankles together.

"Now who's come off second best?" Beegee grinned, rolling Joan on to the bed. "What's wrong, Joanie, cat got your tongue?"

Leaving Joan lying back down on the bed, Beegee went to pick up the dress and put it on. She lifted Joan's vanity bag which had fallen with the clothes and tipped the entire contents into her own bag. After putting on the hat, Beegee came across the room and stood with hands on hips grinning down at Joan.

"Your make-up's all smeared, Joanie," she said and dipped a finger into the pot of rouge on the dressing table, rubbing her finger on the tip of Joan's nose and leaving a red stain. "That's better. Now for some eye-shadow."

By the time Beegee had finished, Joan's nose looked like a clown's and she appeared to have two glorious black eyes. All the time she had struggled and tried to free herself, but failed. At last Beegee stepped back and stood with hands on her hips, admiring her work.

"It's an improvement," she said. "Well, I'm going for a last look at the Buffalo Hide, Joanie. Don't bother to see me out. I'll tell somebody what's happened to you—before I catch the midnight train."

"It's time we went to collect Miss Shandley," Waco drawled, looking at the clock on ths wall.

"Why sure," agreed the Kid. "Ain't that just like a woman, though. She done forgot to tell us which hotel she's staying at."

"It won't be the Bella Union or the Grand," drawled Waco and went to where the floor manager stood. "Where at's Miss Shandley live?"

"Along the street there, at a small hotel down on Crail Street. You turn left here and it's first on the right."

On leaving the saloon Waco and the Kid strolled along the sidewalk towards the junction of Crail Street. Already the town seemed to be waking up, people on the sidewalks going about their business or looking for pleasure. Yet Crail Street, lying just off the main entertainment area of the town, was silent and empty as the two Texans reached it.

"I don't like it," said the Kid. "It's not natural for a chore to go this easy."

"Sure is restful, though," Waco replied. "Coming up here and—say, there's Miss Joan now, new red dress and all."

Ahead of them lay a small hotel, some three buildings down the street, and facing it a livery barn. A small shape in a daring red dress and wide brimmed, flower decorated hat, came from the hotel's front door, showing in the light of the hall lamps.

Even as the two Texans started forward to meet the woman, they saw a couple of dark shapes detach themselves from the shadows by the livery barn. Flame spurted twice from the shapes, the flat crack of shots ringing out. The small shape jerked under the impact of lead and fell against the hitching rail and from there went down.

"Take 'em, boy!" the Kid ordered.

One of the shapes whirled to face the two Texans. He brought up his hand, for they could tell the shape was masculine, sending a bullet from his gun at the advancing Texans.

All in one flickering blur of movement, Waco came to a halt, dipped his right hand, brought out the Army Colt from its holster at his right side and shot at the man. He shot instinctively, without using sights, although the range was greater than most folks would have cared to chance such shooting over. The man who fired at him staggered back a couple of steps; which was good, lucky—or both—shooting on Waco's part. However, the man did not go down, nor did he drop his gun, for he fired again. Raising his Colt shoulder high, Waco shot to kill. He sent a bullet into the man's head and dropped him to the ground.

Ignoring the yells and footsteps on the street behind him, Waco moved forwards, making for where the small shape in the red dress lay sprawled on the edge of the hotel's porch.

The second man had turned and run instead of standing his ground. He reached the safety of the livery barn's end and disappeared down the side alley almost before his pard died.

Leaving Waco to take care of the first man, the Ysabel Kid went after the second. Cold rage filled him as he raced along the alley at the other end of the livery barn. The Kid did not know why the man might have killed Joan Shandley, but he sure as hell did not intend to let him get away with it.

Turning the corner of the building, the Kid saw his man swinging afork a horse. The old Dragoon Colt came from the Kid's holster even as the man reached for the reins of his pard's horse which had been standing by the other animal ready for a quick departure.

"Going someplace?" the Kid asked.

His words brought the man swinging to face him. Up lifted the man's right hand, the left coming across to strike back the Colt he held, hammer and fan off shots.

Fanning might not be the most accurate way to shoot, but it sure as hell could empty a single-action gun faster than any other method. It could also make things real interesting for the man at the wrong end of the gun.

After two bullets narrowly missed him, the shooter showing riding skill in the way he stayed afork his horse by knee-pressure alone, for fanning took both hands, the Kid decided he had had enough. Flinging himself to one side in a rolling dive, the Kid lit down in the shadows of the barn. His black clothing merged with the shadows and yet he, with an almost cat-like ability, could see enough of his man to be able to shoot straight.

The old Dragoon bellowed out like a cannon. A .44 caliber, soft lead ball weighing a third of an ounce was propelled through the seven and a half inch barrel of the Dragoon by the expanding gases of forty grains of black powder. When it struck flesh, such a bullet had a terrible disruptive effect, tearing muscle, sinews and bone. The Kid saw his man thrown bodily from the saddle as his bullet struck home, crash on to the corral fence and slide down it to the ground. Spooked by the shots, the two horses broke away and fled into the darkness.

Coming to his feet, the Kid walked towards the still shape on the ground. He kicked the revolver away from the man's side, but it was only a reflex action, the kind of precaution a man took automatically if he was wise in such matters. One glance told the Kid he did not need to bother about the man, there was no danger in that direction.

A noise and a faint glinting of light sent the Kid gliding into the blackness of the shadows once more. He did not know how the approaching person stood in the matter and so took no chances. Creaking loudly, the livery barn's rear door opened and a scared looking man held out a lantern to peer from the barn.

"Who-all's out there?" he asked in a quavering voice. "And if you-all going to shoot, don't bother. I don't want to know."

"You'd best stay inside," the Kid replied, not showing himself. "There's a dead man out here."

"Ah sure hope that ain't him talking to me, sir. I'm going back inside."

"Give me the lamp first."

Hesitantly, looking ready to drop it at a second's notice, the man extended the lamp and gave a startled jerk as the Kid emerged silently from the shadows and took it.

"You-all the living one, sir?" asked the man.

"I hope so," grinned the Kid. "Man never can tell though."

Thrusting the lamp into the Kid's hand, the man ducked back into the barn and slammed the door. The Kid walked towards the still shape of his victim, hearing feet thudding as people ran along the alley he used to reach the rear of the building.

"Who is he, mister?" asked a voice.

"I'd tell you better happen I'd seen him," the Kid replied and walked to the body. "Any of you know him?"

Some half a dozen or so men stood around in a loose half circle and looked down at the body. A mutter of negative answers came from the crowd. The man's dress was range style, cowhand happen one wanted to be charitable; only he was the sort of cowhand who never worked cattle. A cheap gun-hand, the Kid guessed, the kind who took on at bargain rates and stayed loyal as long as the risks were slight. To the best of his knowledge, the Kid had never seen the man before, only his type.

"Where at's the law?" he asked.

"Saw a deputy coming just as I started to come down here," a man replied.

"I'll go give him the good news."

Not one of the crowd thought of suggesting that the Kid remained where he was until the law got around to seeing him. They parted to allow the tall, slim Texan through, then gathered around to examine the body and comment on its wound.

On the street, the Kid found another crowd gathered and walked towards it. He did not try to force his way through, but swung around the edge and went along the sidewalk to where Waco stood with a deputy from the town marshal's office. The deputy was tall, lean and efficient looking. To the Kid he looked like the kind of tough professional who stayed in office and worked under less able, but better politically backed men.

"I kept everybody back from the body," Waco was saying as the Kid approached. "Could see there was nothing I could do for her, so I let her lie."

Beegee lay face down on the sidewalk, two gaping holes in the left side of her body. Even falling had not dislodged the hat and its pins had held it in place, hiding the blonde hair underneath.

"How'd you know enough about law work to do that?" the deputy asked.

"I was a deputy under Dusty Fog in Mulrooney."

"Huh, huh!" grunted the deputy, studying Waco and deciding he could be that blonde Texas kid who wore a badge in the early days of Mulrooney's existence. "Say this's Beegee Benson!"

"Joan Shandley," Waco contradicted. "She won the hat and red dress off the other gal in a poker game and came here to put it on and red up."

At that moment the town marshal arrived. Bill McBain was a big, heavy man running to fat, with clothes too expensive to have come out of his salary and wearing a Navy Colt which rode too high on his side. All

in all, he looked like a man who knew his place and how
to keep the right folks contented around town.

Elbowing his way importantly through the crowd,
McBain threw a glance around him, saw the reporter—
who was also editor and printer—of the *Newton Daily
News* was on hand, so proceeded to take charge.

"What's all this, Ted?" he asked the deputy. "Who's
been killed?"

"I thought it was Beegee Benson. But this young
feller allows it's Joan Shandley. There's a dead feller
lying on the street. Two holes in him."

"Two killings at one time?" growled McBain as if it
was his deputy's fault.

"Three killings," drawled the Kid, moving forward.
"I dropped his pard back of the livery barn."

Swinging towards the Kid, McBain eyed his lean, wiry
frame and the mocking light in the red hazel eyes. The
Kid was no respecter of persons unless the said persons
rated worthy of his respect. One type of man he disliked
was a lawman who held his post on political ties.

"We'd best look into this," boomed McBain, who
always spoke as if asking a crowd of citizens to vote for
him and expounding his sterling qualities for their inspection.

"Yeah," grunted Ted, the deputy, his tone showing
no respect for his superior's presence or abilities. "Let's
do just that."

"How'd you pair come into this?" McBain went on,
turning to the Texans.

"Let's talk in private," replied the Kid.

"I always believe everything should be done publicly
and openly," McBain answered. "Unless you've
something to——"

Luckily for McBain he did not get around to finishing
his speech. Ted had gone to the side of the dead woman
and bent down to remove the hat. A pile of blonde hair
met his gaze and he looked around at the two Texans.

"Thought you said this was Joan Shandley," he said, cutting McBain's highly undiplomatic speech off.

"Sure I——!" Waco started to reply. "Hell, it's not her."

"Nope," Ted agreed. "Now why should any body want to kill Joan any more'n Beegee, always reckoning anybody wanted to kill either of 'em?"

"I could think of maybe a couple of hundred thousand good reasons, all Yankee dollars," drawled the Kid.

"I don't get it," said the puzzled sounding Ted.

"Maybe somebody didn't want Joan Shandley to get 'em either."

"What Lon's trying to say, him talking Comanche and all," Waco said, "is that Elmo Thackery left Joan some of his money in his will; equal share with six other folks. Only maybe there's one or more of 'em greedy and wanted more'n their seventh share."

"Where at's Joan now?" Ted asked. "If she come home to change into these duds, how come Beegee was wearing them?"

"Up in her room'd be a good place to try looking," grunted the Kid.

Nodding, Ted started to turn. The trouble was McBain outranked him and the marshal, with an eye on the forthcoming elections, did not intend to let a chance to make a grandstand play slip through his fingers. He had a fair-sized crowd and a newspaperman on hand. Although he had never heard of it, McBain knew the value of newspaper publicity to a campaigning officer. So he wanted to parade his authority in plain view, and did not like the idea of one of his deputies making any of the decisions.

"Now just a minute!" he snapped. "Before we start traipsing off, let's have us some frank talk. What'd you pair come to Newton for?"

"To tell Joan Shandley that she'd been left money in

Elmo Thackery's will," replied the Kid.

"You work for Thackery?"

"For Ole Devil Hardin. Thackery's lawyer asked Ole Devil to get us boys out to find the folks who get a cut of the will."

"Who're you?" McBain growled.

"Loncey Dalton Ysabel."

"The Ysabel Kid?"

"I've been called worse. This's Waco."

"And you brought Joan news that she'd inherited a fortune. How did you know where to find her?"

"Pinkerton located her for the old man. We came here on their word."

"There'd be a lot of money involved," McBain said loudly. "Enough for the other folks maybe not to want a saloongirl to cut in."

"There's mean folks all over the world, even in Texas," the Kid replied. "Only we didn't kill her, then shoot those two fellers for them to take the blame."

"Nobody said you did!"

"It's a thought though, isn't it?"

McBain did not reply. He did take a hurried step to the rear as the Kid's right hand dropped and lifted the big old Dragoon from the holster. However, the Kid did not grip the revolver's butt, but held it by the chamber and offered it to Ted.

"There's only one shot fired," he told the deputy. "Which same I use loose powder and ball."

"Here, I put two out, into that feller," Waco went on, handing over his guns to McBain. "And there was folks right up close after I fired."

The implications were obvious. Beegee had been killed by two bullets, the man on the street had two wounds, making a total of four shots; five at least if the Ysabel Kid spoke truly about there being another dead man behind the livery barn. The two Texans had expended only three shots between them; the very least they could have got by with, even discounting the man behind the barn, was four. Nor would they have had time to reload before the crowd arrived and saw them doing so. Which meant they most likely told the truth.

"No offence meant," he said, for showing he could admit he might have been wrong had its value properly handled. "A law enf——"

"Hey!" Waco interrupted, taking and holstering his Colts. "If Beegee's down here wearing Joan's clothes, where at's Joan?"

"Her hotel room's the most likely place," replied Ted. "Let's go up there and see."

"Yeah, let's," agreed the Kid. "How's about tending to moving the bodies, marshal? The tax payers don't want their street cluttering up, do they?"

Before McBain could make any reply, the three men had entered the hotel where an old man who acted as reception clerk told them the number of Joan's room. McBain scowled after his deputy, then shrugged and exercised his authority by ordering men to carry the bodies to the undertaker's shop.

After knocking a couple of times without a reply, the men were about to look elsewhere for Joan, when they heard her feet bumping on the floor. Bursting open the door, they found Joan, looking dishevelled, sitting on her bed still securely bound and with a gag in her mouth.

"Where is she?" Joan spluttered as soon as Waco unfastened the gag. "I'll yank her blonde hair out by its black roots."

"Who?" asked the Kid.

"Beegee Benson, that's who! I'll take——"

"You didn't hear the shooting?" asked the deputy, then decided that would be impossible as the room was at the back of the building.

"Shooting?" Joan gasped, drawing her cloak around her on being cut free. "What shooting?"

"Beegee was shot as she left the hotel," the Kid told her bluntly.

Joan looked at the three faces. Nobody would joke about such a thing, and their faces sure didn't look like they were joking.

"Beegee—— Oh no! Who did it?"

"Couple of fellers, looked like cheap hired gunmen. We got them both."

Although the Kid's statement that they had got the men did not bring Beegee back, it made Joan feel a little bitter. She looked at the men, her grief showing even though she fought to hide it.

"Who did this to you?" Waco asked, lighting the room's lamp and then closing the door.

"Beegee."

"Beegee?" growled the Kid.

"Sure. We were getting tired of this town and set to move on. So Beegee got the jump on me before I could nail her, or tell her about my good luck."

"You'd best explain that to us," Ted remarked, sounding puzzled.

"Sure. It's been going on between Beegee and me for a few—all right, for at least fifteen years. Whenever we got together in the same saloon we'd try to leave town with each other's best dress and jewelry. One time I told the boss girl that Beegee had been calling her names, and left town with all Beegee's clothes, except for an old dress while they were fighting. Another time Beegee got word to some tough mick railroad worker's wife that he and I were having fun. I wasn't in shape to stop Beegee taking off with a new feather boa and everything but five dollars and a gingham dress that I owned. We didn't mean anything by it. I'd slipped Beegee a drink from the little green bottle under the bar one time, got away with everything except what she stood up in, or lay under the table in. It was six months later that Beegee caught up with me—and I was down with fever and flat broke. Beegee worked and kept me, got me well again. Then when she bust her leg in a stagecoach crash, I left a good job in a Texas saloon to go take care of her and pay her doctor's fees.''

"She grateful for it?" asked Waco.

"Sure. Three months later we fought for nearly half an hour when she found I'd taken a rich feller she aimed to talk into buying her a hat shop. That was some fight, I'll tell you. The boss of the saloon offered a hundred bucks each to have another when we got over the first. But we'd made it up by then and found us another town.''

The men watched Joan, realizing she was only talking to keep herself from breaking down and crying. For the first time they noticed the make-up smeared on Joan's face. Under other circumstances it would have been amusing, but none of the men felt like laughing. They knew Beegee had been Joan's friend, despite all they did to each other, and nobody found anything to do with losing a friend funny.

"But who'd want to kill Beegee?" Joan asked, rubbing her face with the edge of her cloak. "She was always such good fun and didn't have an enemy in the world. She never rolled a drunk, or raised a man's hopes and then let him down. Everybody liked her.''

"How about you?" Waco asked.

"I liked her, she was my friend."

"I mean did you have any enemies?"

For a long moment Joan looked at the young Texan. Then her mind started to follow the way his led. Quite a number of people had seen Beegee lose the red dress and fancy hat, then heard Joan say she intended to go to the hotel and dress in it. Only Beegee beat her to it and left the hotel wearing the dress and hat. Beegee who was so much like Joan, except for her blonde hair which the hat hid from sight.

"Do you think those men might've been waiting for me?" she asked.

"They were waiting for somebody, that's for sure. And they wouldn't shoot a woman down without real good reason."

"It was light enough for them to know they were cutting down a woman," the Kid went on, following Waco's train of thought and not liking the conclusions emerging from it.

"But who'd want to kill me?" Joan groaned. "Where is B—the—where is——"

"Marshal's had it moved to the undertaker's," Ted answered.

"Look boys," Joan said, turning to the Texans. "That letter you gave me said I could draw up to two thousand dollars against the Thackery money if I wanted, didn't it?"

"So Lawyer Talbot told us," agreed the Kid.

"I'd like to get it and give Beegee a good burying. I aimed to cut her in on whatever I got and I'd like to know she was buried decent."

"You'll have to wait until the bank opens in the morning," the Kid said. "You had any bad fuss with anybody recently?"

"Never. Sure I've had a few hair yankings and screaming matches with other girls, but nothing serious," Joan replied. "Who else is sharing that money with me?"

"Kin folks mostly, I reckon," the Kid replied. "Knowing Elmo Thackery he wouldn't cut in too many folks."

"Do you think one of them might——" Joan began, then stopped, for she did not know how to carry on.

"That could be," admitted the Kid.

"It'd have to be somebody at Casa Thackery though," Waco put in. "None of the folks we're gathering would know about Joan or how to find her."

"Yeah," the Kid answered. "I'm going down to the saloon to ask one of the girls to come spend the night with you, Joan. Then comes morning, you're not leaving either me or Waco's sight for a minute, 'cepting when you have to go someplace where we can't follow, and even then we'll be outside.''

"Do you think they might try at me again?" she asked.

"I don't know," the Kid replied. "But I sure as hell don't want to face Dusty happen they do try—and bring it off.''

CHAPTER FOUR

Mark Counter Meets Mr. And
Mrs. Claude Thackery

"Move your feet afore I kick 'em from under you!"

Mark Counter reached up a hand to shove back his hat and look at the speaker, hoping against hope that his ears were playing tricks on him.

They were not. The speaker stood with hands on hips, legs braced apart and body riding the swaying of the railroad coach with the ease of a horseman on a smooth moving mount.

A cavalry kepi perched on short, curly red hair and a friendly, happy face looked down at him. Although the speaker wore a fringed buckskin jacket, open necked cavalry shirt, red silk bandana tight knotted and rolled at the throat to trail its ends over the shirt, buckskin pants, high heeled riding boots and an ivory handled Navy Colt rode butt forward in the holster at the right side, nobody—unless very short-sighted—would have taken it for a man.

As usual Calamity Jane's shirt and pants looked as if they had been bought two sizes too tight. Since they had last met, Calamity appeared to have put on a bit of weight, although she still slimmed down at the middle without the aid of corsets. She had a full, mature figure which would catch the eye in any company.

"Hello, Calam," Mark growled and drew down his hat once more. "Good-bye."

"Now is that the way a Southern gentleman greets a

lady?'' asked Calamity, flopping on the seat facing him and dropping her blacksnake whip beside her. "Anybody's reckon you aren't pleased to see me."

"I'm not."

"You sure?" Calamity grinned.

Thrusting back his hat, Mark sat up and looked at the girl. Then he grinned just as broadly.

"It wouldn't do any good if I said I was. How've you been keeping, Calam?"

"Fit as a flea. I only just caught the train and come through here to see if there was anybody I knew aboard, and danged me if I don't find you."

"Why sure, Calam girl, it must be fate."

"If it's fate, then fate's sure got a hate for me," Calamity answered with a smile that lit up her face. "Seems every time I meet up with you I wind up rolling on the floor with some gal trying to scalp me barehanded."

"How about me?" Mark objected. "Last time we met I wound up wrestling down a couple of bullwhackers."

"And that sure was a dilly of a brawl," Calamity chuckled, for her boasting of Mark's strength and fighting ability brought the business about and mixed a saloon's crowd in the general brawl that followed Mark's effective handling of the pair of bull-whackers.

"It sure was. Where you headed, Calamity gal?"

"For the construction camp at the railhead. I've been freighting for the railroad meat hunters, but Buffalo Bill's got him some English lord or something to take out on a big hunt and wants me along. How about you?"

"I'm headed to the same place——"

"To go hunting with Bill?" Calamity gasped.

"Nope. I'm looking for a feller called Claude Thackery."

For a long moment Calamity did not speak, but her eyes studied the big Texan's face. One way and another

Calamity Jane knew Mark Counter pretty well. They had been good friends for several years and had sided each other in a couple of tight corners. Calamity reckoned she knew when Mark was funning her, and he did not appear to be doing so at the moment.

"I wouldn't have thought *you*'d want to see *him*!" she finally said. "You've never become one of them, have you?"

"One of what, gal?" grinned Mark.

"One of them stinking socialists, or whatever they call themselves! That bunch who come out of them fancy eastern colleges and start dripping brotherly love over us uncouth, horny-handed workers, hating our guts all the time but willing to use us happen it'll get them what they want."

"What do they want, gal?"

"Everything anybody's worked hard to get and that's showing a profit. *You* surely haven't joined them."

Mark grinned. His father owned the biggest ranch in the Texas Big Bend country; one built by hard work and because Big Ranse Counter was smarter and more able than the other men around. Where they had been content to let Big Ranse take the responsibility and risks of ownership, they played safe and accepted wages. The way Mark looked at it, his old man had worked damned hard for what he got and had the right to hang on to it, not hand it over to folks who had been willing to sit back and take his pay while he built his spread up.

"Nope. I'm going to collect him for his old man, 'lease to get a share of his old man's will."

"Had you asked me," sniffed Calamity, "I'd've said Thackery's maw and paw only met the one time."

"And I'd say you're a vulgar, uncouth young lady for thinking such thoughts, Calam," Mark grinned.

One of the reasons he liked Calamity was her complete disregard for the conventions which bound the womenfolk of their day. Calamity lived the way she liked, said what she pleased, and stood full willing to back her words if called on them. She certainly showed no offence or anger at his comment, merely throwing back her head and laughing merrily.

"Aren't I though?" she said. "And I'm a good cook with it."

"Why sure you are, Calam. And the way to a man's heart is through his stomach they do say."

"I've got me a skillet in the caboose," Calamity remarked, then became serious again. "Are you for real coming up here after Thackery?"

"Why else?"

"Him and his kind's been riling up the railroad bosses with their trouble-causing and rabble-rousing. They've been causing unrest among the track-laying gangs with all their talk about all men being equal and having the right to share their hands on everything other folks have had brains enough to build."

"You reckon I've taken to selling my guns now, Calamity?"

"No I don't. Only the railroad bosses can play rough when they have to. The last Socialist who came up here flapping his lip left faster'n he come."

"Alive?" Mark asked.

"Sure. You don't have to lean heavy on scum like that. Speak a mite rough to them and they run screaming for the law to protect them. Funny thing about that is they can't say a good word for the law any other time."

"And you figure they're thinking of leaning on Thackery a mite?"

"I don't know," admitted Calamity. "When I came down to Newton on the train Thackery was expected, but hadn't arrived. All I know is that the railroad bosses aren't fixing in to have him or his sort talk the construction gangs into any more delays, and they know a helluva lot of ways to make a man mighty unhappy if they don't like him." She paused and looked out of the window, watching the rolling plains fall behind them.

"Say, how's Cap'n Dusty, the Kid and all the folks?"

And so the subject of Thackery became shelved to let them talk about mutual friends and discover what each had been doing since their last meeting. While they talked, and wondered how they might put this chance meeting to its fullest advantage, the train carried them west towards the forward construction base camp which had been erected to supply the needs of the ever-advancing steel rails.

Night was falling as the train halted at the depot, if a single canvas-walled shack could be glorified by such a grand title. Calamity and Mark were among the first to leave the train and they stood side by side, looking around them.

A fair-sized town stretched before them. It had homes, stores, saloons, a dance hall and a couple of gambling palaces; all of them made of canvas. The railroad had now stretched too far west to make the building of a more permanent town worthwhile at this point. They were well beyond the range where Texas trail drives would come to ship their cattle. So the people erected canvas structures which could be taken down and transported to the next base camp when the present camp fell so far behind the construction that it was useless for its purpose.

"I'll just go ask the——" Calamity began, then chopped off her words as she glanced along the train. "Ho, ho! I thought they might be along."

"Who?" Mark answered.

"Why those three jaspers getting down from the coach ahead."

Turning, Mark looked to where a couple of big, burly toughs followed a much smaller man from the far end of the next coach. They all wore derby hats and town suits, but the bigger pair had gunbelts under their coats and tied down holsters. Even though the light was none too good, Mark could tell the two big men had surly mean faces and the shorter carried himself with the swaggering, cocky assurance of a small *hombre* with plenty of authority and power behind him.

"Who are they, Calam?" he asked.

"That lil feller's all I know for sure. His name's Sam Strogoff and he's one of Pinkerton's top men. Other two work for him. I've seen them around when there's been trouble on the railroad afore. And brother, when they left, there's mostly been heads broken among the trouble-causers."

That figured happen a man believed all he heard about the activities of the Pinkerton Agency when handling labor disputes for their employers. Mark, as became a stout Confederate sympathizer, had little respect for Pinkertons, but he kept an open mind as to whether they were as black as a lot of folks painted them.

"Reckon they're here after Thackery?" he inquired.

"Could be," Calamity admitted.

"Who-all's the head man up here?" Mark went on. "When we ran the law in Mulrooney last year it was Phil Chaseman."

"Still is. You'll know him then?"

"Well enough, Calam. Where do I find him?"

"I'll take you to him," Calamity promised. "Just let me go tell the train conductor to keep my gear until I collect it."

"I'm working this trip, Calam," Mark warned grimly. "I don't want to wind up in any saloon brawl. You hear me, gal?"

"I hear you good," she replied. "And Bill's told me there's no job for me happen I make trouble. I like a fight, but I like money good, too."

Mark eyed Calamity suspiciously. Like the Ysabel Kid, Calamity was never to be trusted when she sounded as innocent as a church-pew full of choirboys. Dropping a big right hand on her shoulder, his left held his bedroll, Mark gave the girl's flesh a squeeze which made her wince in pain.

"Just mind you do, Calam girl," he warned. "Because if you don't I'll take down your pants and paddle your bare hide."

Rubbing her numb shoulder, Calam looked at Mark in a challenging manner.

"Is that a threat or a promise?" she asked. "And don't tell me here, wait until later."

After seeing the conductor of the train and arranging for the safe keeping of her belongings, Calamity joined Mark. They walked along the railroad track and under a romantic starlit sky, yet they did not speak of romance.

"I've found where Thackery's going to speak tonight," she said. "Asked the depot agent."

"Where?" Mark inquired. "Did I hurt your shoulder?"

"Naw. I always start every day by letting a hoss walk on it. He'll be at O'Sullivan's Load."

"Where's that?"

"The big place over to the back of town," Calamity explained. "Swell place, considering the walls are made of canvas. Right strange name it's got, though."

"Yeah," Mark agreed. "Real strange. All right, you've got me interested. Why'd they call it O'Sullivan's Load?"

Calamity explained and Mark began to grin. An idea formed in his head, just tentatively, of how he could get Thackery alone for long enough to tell him about his father's death, which probably would not interest him; and the fact that he inherited a share of the money which almost certainly would.

"Only one thing though," Calamity drawled, cutting in on Mark's thoughts. "The depot agent don't reckon Thackery's going to be in very good shape if he goes through with this speechifying tonight. That's what Strogoff and his boys have come up here to tend to."

"Is, huh?" Mark answered.

"Why sure. There's Chaseman's private car, up ahead."

On establishing this spot as a base camp, the railroad officials had caused several sidings to be built from the main tracks. Here in safety, stood the mobile offices, the big cars which would move on when another camp be fixed farther west. As befitted the senior official present, Chaseman's car stood in its own siding. Only the nearest end of the long car had light at the windows and Mark saw the big, bulky silhouette of Chaseman pass one of the windows, he appeared to be pacing up and down restlessly. From what Mark could remember, that meant Chaseman had a difficult decision to make. Mark could even hazard a guess at what the decision had to do with.

Seeing the two big Pinkerton men lounging by the lit end of the wagon, Mark knew, or felt reasonably certain, his guess was correct.

"That's the one," Calamity announced unnecessarily. "Want me along?"

"Thought you'd work to do?"

"Naw. Not until late tomorrow. Say those two Pinkertons are waiting."

"Why sure. Stay on here, Calam. I'll go talk to them."

One thing Calamity had learned early was not to argue with Mark when his voice took on that quiet, but grim note. She knew Mark expected trouble in getting to see Chaseman and the only menace she could see was the two burly Pinkerton men who lounged by the lit end of the car. While figuring Mark could take care of the two men, Calamity uncoiled her whip and flipped its long lash behind her. A girl lost nothing by being ready for any emergency.

Warbag in hand, Mark walked towards the railroad car, Calamity trailing on his heels, but a few feet behind him. The car's lit window had been raised a little and he could hear Chaseman's voice.

"I don't like it, Strogoff."

"Your head office does," came a reply.

"They aren't out here. All you'll do is ma——"

"Where do you reckon you're going, cow-nurse?" asked the bigger of the two men, thrusting himself from the side of the car to block Mark's path.

"To see Phil Chaseman."

"He's busy," the second man stated, ranging himself alongside his pard. "At least that's what he told us, ain't it, Sid?"

"That's what he told us all right, Meyer," the bigger man agreed. "Go 'way and come back in morning, please honorable cownurse."

"I'll see him right now," Mark drawled and Calamity tensed, for she knew the note which crept into the big Texan's voice.

"You will, huh?" Meyer grunted, moving forward. "We'll see about th——"

His words ended abruptly as Mark's heavy bedroll rose into the air and drove out to crash into his chest, staggering him backwards.

Sid had been taken just as much by surprise as had Meyer. Seeing his partner stagger backwards, Sid prepared to take action against the big Texan. However, the taking of action needed quick thought. Guns were out, that was for sure. Sid knew his limitations and could guess that any attempt at gunplay would see him wind up second best. Nor had he failed to notice the casual manner in which Mark raised the bedroll and tossed it into Meyer's face. A man that strong needed real strong measures taken against him.

With that thought in mind, Sid dipped his right hand into his jacket pocket instead of at his gun butt. In the pocket, his fingers found the holes of a set of brass knuckledusters. Sid made the move with the easy skill of long practice and without any fumbling. His hand entered his pocket empty and came out bearing a deadly brass armoury sheathing his knuckles ready to rip the big Texan's face out of shape.

Only he reckoned without Mark's ingrained objections to having the shape of his face altered.

Catching a faint glinting of light on the hand which emerged from Sid's pocket, and knowing the man was not wearing rings which might have caused it, Mark guessed what Sid planned to do. Mark also took exception to the plan. Stepping forward fast, Mark drove out his left fist, throwing a punch with all his weight behind it into Sid's belly. Sid had never been kicked in the belly by a mule, but after the blow he was in a position to describe how it would feel to take a mule's kick. All his breath went in a croaking, agonized gasp as he doubled over.

Up lashed Mark's right hand, driving under Sid's unprotected jaw with a crack like two lumps of rock colliding together. Sid abruptly changed direction. Instead of going downwards, his head and shoulders shot erect and his body, already moving backwards, flew to the rear and smashed into the side of the car. Like twin heat-buckled candles, Sid's legs buckled under him. His eyes glazed over and he tumbled forward on to his face.

Having dealt with Sid, Mark swung around to handle the menace that Meyer ought by this time to be offering him. He found his fears groundless and his attentions not needed, for Meyer had troubles of his own.

On landing hard upon his rump, Meyer began to spit out curses and saw Sid's hand dip into the pocket. Knowing what Sid's pocket carried, Meyer did not think he would be needed; except to help put a boot into the unconscious Texan's body. Then he saw that the Texan was not the one rendered unconscious and so jerked the Adam's revolver from its holster. Having seen the efficient way in which the Texan handled Sid, Meyer did not aim to take any chances.

Calamity had stayed in the shadows, watching what happened. She did not doubt that Mark could handle both men and saw no reason to spoil his fun. Watching Mark fight was both enjoyable and instructive. Calamity had learned more than one trick from Mark's repertoire that came in useful to her at some later date.

Then she saw Meyer start to draw his gun and knew Mark would not have finished with Sid in time to take the appropriate counter measures. Swinging up her arm, Calamity raised the whip's lash and sent it coiling out. Nor did she use the whip gently, for Calamity had no love of Pinkerton men. Out curled the lash, wrapping around Meyer's wrist even as he raised the gun, jerking savagely at it.

Meyer yelled in agony, feeling as if his wrist had been broken in the crushing grip of the whip's lash. Grabbing with his left hand, Meyer caught the lash and hauled on it with all his strength. He not only felt the grip on his injured wrist relax, but hauled the whip-wielder bodily towards him. Having seen how comparatively small and slight Calamity looked, Meyer prepared to drive his left fist into flesh when the girl came into range.

In all fairness to Meyer it must be stated he did not at that point know Calamity was a girl. To be truthful, the knowledge would not have changed his plan in the slightest. When he was hurt, Meyer's instincts always led him to hurt back and he did not care who received the injury.

So, although his Adams had fallen from a numb and useless hand, Meyer still determined to fight back. By heaving on the whip's lash he hoped to bring the figure at the other end into range where he could strike at it.

He got his wish—although not quite in the manner he hoped for.

Feeling herself hauled forward, Calamity prepared to use an old whip-fighter's trick she had learned from a freighter. Although Meyer thought his pull alone propelled the girl towards him, Calamity was running forward and measuring the distance with her eye. Just as Meyer prepared to send his fist smashing up between Calamity's legs, she made her move. Up lashed her foot, the riding boot's toe catching Meyer under the chin. Calamity had a shapely pair of legs, as Mark well knew,

but they were also legs packed with powerful muscles
and she knew how to get the best out of them.

Calamity timed her kick just right, it lifted the man's
rump a foot from the ground, snapped his head over
almost hard enough to break his neck, and sent him flat
on to his back. He landed sprawled out, arms thrown
wide and without making any movement.

"Thanks, Calam honey," Mark grinned.

"Behind you!" she yelled, her right hand twisting
palm out and bringing up the Navy Colt, the whip
falling to her feet.

Turning fast, Mark's right hand brought its Colt
from leather, clicked back the hammer under an
educated thumb and lined it up to where Strogoff and
Chaseman stood on the platform of the car.

The fact that two guns now covered him changed
Strogoff's intention of drawing his Colt Cloverleaf
House Pistol from under his jacket. Having heard the
noise outside the car, Strogoff and Chaseman came
hurriedly to investigate. Seeing his two men flattened
in such a manner brought a desire for revenge to
Strogoff's heart, but not such a strong one that he
would risk his own hide to take it.

"Just stand like that, *hombre*," Mark told Strogoff,
then glanced at Chaseman. "You're a hard man to get
to see, Phil."

"It's Mark Counter, isn't it?" Chaseman replied.

The head of the construction camp looked much the
same as when Mark last saw him, a big, burly man, hard
as nails under the frilly fronted white shirt and city style
pants he wore around his office. His face held a warm,
welcoming smile which clashed with the scowl Strogoff
directed at the big Texan after looking at the two unconscious toughs.

"What the hell happened here?" Strogoff snarled,
before Mark could answer Chaseman's greeting.

"Some folks just don't know when to get tough,
hombre," Mark answered. "And I don't take to a man

pulling brass knuckles on me. Can I come in and talk, Phil?"

"Any time, Mark. Hi, Calamity, you in on this?"

"Why sure. That other feller, the one with the gun by him, was all set to throw down on Mark from behind, so I asked him not to."

Angry growls came from Strogoff's throat, but he did not direct any of his thoughts into words. In his own way Strogoff could be a hard citizen, but he was far out of his own way now. Those two unconscious toughs proved that.

"Come on in, Mark, bring Calamity with you. You'd best see to your men, Strogoff. I'll talk to you about this business of yours later."

"I'm one against three here," Strogoff growled. "Alan's not going to like it when he gets my report."

"You tell him what your boys did to wind up like that, and tell him true. I aim to in my report," Chaseman answered.

Still growling angrily, Strogoff stamped down the steps and pushed by Mark to walk towards the groaning Meyer. Mark picked up his bedroll and Calamity lifted and coiled her whip.

"Meyer's wrist's sprained and it looks like his jaw's broke," Strogoff snarled, looking up at Chaseman.

"He'll know better'n try to hit a lady next time," Calamity answered. "You look at the other one, Strogoff, I bet he don't feel too good either."

On examination it was proved that Meyer had a sprained wrist, but his jaw was not broken, although he did not feel like eating for a couple of days. Nor did Sid—his jaw *was* broken. Which left Strogoff without the support he needed to carry out the work he had been sent to do.

Chaseman left Strogoff to attend to his men, showing Mark and Calamity into his car. The railroad company had done their construction boss proud in the matter of accommodation. The front compartment of his car, into which he showed his visitors, served as a meeting room for Chaseman and was comfortably furnished.

"Take a seat, Calamity, Mark," Chaseman said and waved a hand to the bar in the corner of the room. "What can I get you to drink?"

"Whisky for me, please," Mark replied.

"I'll take a little snort of red-eye myself," Calamity went on. "Whooee, you sure live well."

"So I've been hearing from some of my mick construction workers. One of them wanted to know why I could have a car like this and he couldn't."

"What'd you tell him?" grinned Mark.

"Asked him if he reckoned he could run the camp. He said he couldn't. So I told him that when he got to where he could, then he'd have a car like this to work in. I think he took the point. What brings you up here, Mark?"

"Thackery."

Lowering the bottle from which he was pouring drinks, Chaseman looked hard at Mark, then threw a glance towards the door of the car. He walked across the room and lowered the window through which Mark had overheard some of his conversation with Strogoff.

"What about Thackery?" Chaseman asked.

"How'd you like to get him out of your hair?" Mark drawled.

"I'd like it fine," Chaseman admitted, bringing two glasses of whisky to his guests. "So would head office. That's why they sent Strogoff and his men up here. This's between us, don't forget."

"We won't," Mark promised.

"You've got my word on it," Calamity went on.

With any other woman Chaseman might not have been so keen to believe a promise of silence, but he knew Calamity never broke her word, and also that she knew how to keep her mouth shut.

"I'm against shutting Thackery up that way," Chaseman confessed. "It only makes a martyr of him. Brutal railroad company abuses defender of the poor workers, silences freedom of speech. You know the sort of things some of the Eastern newspapers would say.''

"I'll get rid of him for you, Phil," Mark drawled, sipping appreciatively at his drink. "Man, that came from the real bottle."

"It sure did," agreed Calamity. "You listen to Mark, Phil. He's got him a jim-dandy idea for getting rid of Thackery."

"How?" Chaseman asked.

"My way," Mark replied.

A grin creased Chaseman's face. Back in Mulrooney he had seen Mark Counter in action. Even though Mark had been suffering from a shoulder wound during the early days Dusty Fog held office as town marshal, it did not prevent Mark taking his fair share of the work load.

Now Mark had no injury to slow him down, but Chaseman wondered what brought the big Texan out on to the plains so far from the Rio Hondo country and apparently looking for Claude Thackery.

It could be for political reasons, the newly formed Socialist Party being frowned on by the Democrats. Mark voted for the Democratic Party, what Texan did not? Yet he had never been so closely involved in the Party's political activities that he would go out of his way to remove a member of some rival organization.

Voices sounded faintly from outside the window, muffled yet showing surprise at what the speakers saw. A few seconds after the car's doors burst open and Strogoff entered.

"Both my men are out of action!" he snapped. "I'm taking out a warrant against this pair, Chaseman."

"They started the fussing!" Calamity replied hotly, coming to her feet.

"From what I heard and saw, Calamity's telling the truth," Chaseman went on. "I saw the brass knuckles Sid was wearing, and the gun by Meyer's side. Was you to ask me, I'd say Mark and Calamity had a good case for assault against your men, if it comes to going to law."

"All right!" snarled Strogoff. "I see I'm one against three again. But Alan won't like it, and neither will your bosses, Chaseman."

"Maybe not. It's been a long time since I last cared what Alan Pinkerton thought, and the bosses have locked horns with me before now. Take your boys to the hospital car, there's a doctor aboard and he'll tend to them."

Strogoff spun on his heel and stamped towards the door of the room. Just before he left, the man turned and scowled back at Calamity and Mark in a threatening manner.

"I've a long memory," he warned.

"Then use it," Mark replied quietly, yet his voice held Strogoff like a bug pinned to a card. "If anything happens to Calamity, like she has an accident, I'll come looking for you and I'll nail your hide to a wall."

"I reckon I can stand up for myself, Mark," Calamity put in. "And Mr. Strogoff'd best mind it. If I lose any freight work, or have any fuss, I'll save Mark the job."

Directing a snarling blanket curse at Calamity, Mark and Chaseman, Strogoff turned and left the room, slamming the door behind him.

"You've made a bad enemy there," Chaseman warned as they heard Strogoff snarling orders outside the car.

"I never had a good one yet," grinned Calamity and sat down to finish her drink.

"How do you reckon to handle Thackery, Mark?" the railroad man asked.

"Easy, provided I get him alone and can whisper a few words in his ear," Mark replied, winking at Calamity. "And don't look so all-fired worried, Phil. I don't aim to kill him, or even threaten him. But I'll bet you a hundred dollars that he'll take the morning train with me and you'll never be troubled by him again."

Seeing that Chaseman still had doubts, Mark explained his plan. Chaseman thought about it for a moment, wondering if such a fool scheme could work. Then he looked Mark over and thought back to the old days in Mulrooney. If any man could make that crackbrained scheme work, that man was Mark Counter.

"Mind if I come along?" he asked. "I'm coming, mind or not."

"Then feel free to join us," Mark replied. "There's only one thing I want for you to do, if I pull this off."

"What's that?" Chaseman asked, and when Mark told him stared his disbelief. Giving a shrug, he agreed to Mark's terms. "I'll do it, Mark, but I sure hope the word never gets back to the head office that I have."

Taken any way a man looked at it, the O'Sullivan's Load Saloon was quite a place. In fact, considering the limitations of being built so that it could be transported when the base camp moved, the saloon could be said to equal the best many a good sized town could offer.

The bar was mahogany, built in sections for easy removal. All the fittings were of good quality, including a crystal chandelier which suspended from a specially strengthened central support. There were gambling tables, the liquor supply catered for all tastes, comfortable chairs for the customers, a bandstand and a stage large enough to present a decent show on it. Several gaily dressed and attractive girls spread their charms among the customers, the waiters were efficient and the bouncers capable.

All this the saloon had—and O'Sullivan's Load.

It stood before the bar on a floor of solid unpolished oak; an enormous iron dumb-bell with a sign before it. The sign announced for all to see, if they could read, the legend of O'Sullivan's Load.

"O'SULLIVAN'S LOAD," the sign read. "On the night of April 19th, 1865, while celebrating the end of the Civil War, the great Seamus O'Sullivan did lift this dumb-bell and raise it to arms' length over his head.

"I, Thomas Barraclough, owner of the O'Sullivan's Load Saloon, do promise to pay any man who can equal O'Sullivan's feat of strength the sum of ONE HUNDRED dollars. I will also supply all who witness a repetition of the feat with free drinks until midnight on the day it is performed."

Standing on a raised dais usually occupied by the saloon's band, Claude Thackery ignored the offer. For one thing he did not have the strength necessary to do anything about it; for another, he was busily engaged in making an impassioned speech on the subject of the equality of men.

Thackery was a tall, thin man with a pinched, mean-looking face that bore a strong resemblance to his father's except that Claude's complexion tended to be sallow and unhealthy. He did not wear a hat and his long hair hung straight back on his thin skull. Usually he wore a better suit, but not when speaking to the workers about equality. His white shirt was grubby and the red tie hung limp on it.

One reason he spoke in the O'Sullivan's Load saloon was that his wife Marlene saw its owner and arranged for him to do so. Marlene was good at arranging such matters. While he went out to speak, she remained in their hotel room, or in this case a borrowed tent. Thackery could not see the owner of the saloon present, but did not care. Barraclough was not promising party material any way.

"The conditions under which you live and work are worse than those of the slaves we freed in the Civil War!" he told the attentive crowd, forgetting that his sole contribution to the Union cause had been making patriotic speeches many miles from the fighting area. "It is time you stood firm and demanded your rights!"

At that moment Calamity Jane, Mark Counter and Phil Chaseman entered the well-lit room. Almost

instantly Thackery found his audience began to lose
interest in his words of wisdom. Some, on seeing the big
boss of the railroad, assumed expressions of complete
disbelief at what Thackery was saying; others turned
their attention from the politician completely.

"Is that sign true?" Mark asked the bartender who
came to take their orders on their arrival at the counter.

"Yep, sure is," the man replied. "The moment she's
hoisted up overhead, the money'll be paid and the
drinks start to flow."

Turning from the bar, Mark walked forward and
stepped on to the boards. He tested them carefully,
making sure they were firm and would not move under
him. Satisfied on this point, Mark examined the huge
dumb-bell and guessed at its weight. If that O'Sullivan
gent raised it over his head, he must have been a
tolerable strong and powerful feller for it would weigh
all of five hundred pounds.

All eyes went to the big Texan, noticing the way he
examined the boards and studied the dumb-bell.
Thackery might have been talking to the walls for all the
notice anybody took of him. Slowly his voice trailed off
and he stood on the dais with his mouth hanging open
speechlessly.

Unbuckling his gunbelt, Mark handed it and his Stetson to Chaseman. Much to Mark's surprise Calamity
had not followed them from the bar, but stood near to
the bartender. Mark wondered why Calamity did not
join him, for it was unlike her to miss a chance of being
at the center of an attraction. Stripping off his shirt, to
many admiring female and male glances, Mark handed
it to Chaseman.

Now Thackery was completely forgotten as the crowd
studied the great spread of Mark's shoulders, the
powerful muscles writhing under his tanned skin, the
enormous biceps, the swelling forearms and large,
strong-fingered hands. Some of the crowd recognized
Mark from the old days in Mulrooney and others could

recall hearing Texan cowhands boast of the blond giant's strength.

One of the house gamblers, on being asked if he would take bets, threw an inquiring look at the bartender. Although he nodded his agreement, the bartender felt worried. A jerk of his head brought one of the waiters to him.

"Go get the boss," he ordered.

"I thought Tom didn't want disturbing until just afore that dude stopped his lip-flapping," the waiter objected.

"Go get him!" snapped the bartender. "I'll take the responsibility." Then, as the waiter hurried away, leaned on the bar top and called to Mark. "Hey, friend, don't you go lift it afore the boss gets here. Wouldn't want you to have to do it twice in one night."

From the bandstand, Thackery saw the crowd settle down again and wondered if he could attract their attention. Before he could start to speak, although he did not feel like chancing speaking while the head man of the camp stood in the same room, he had the matter taken out of his hands.

Stepping to where a girl sat at one of the tables, Mark bent over and whispered a request in her ear. She looked startled, but drew her chair clear of the table and sat on it grinning self-consciously.

The crowd fell silent, watching and wondering what Mark intended to do. He did not keep them in suspense. Bending, he gripped the chair's back legs and started to lift it from the floor. The girl gave a squeal that was part delight at being the center of attraction, and part fear. As the chair rose, she grabbed at its seat and clung on with both hands, her legs kicking out before her.

Lifting the girl and the chair at arms' length and shoulder high, Mark took a couple of steps forward and set them down gently on the table. To laughter and applause from the onlookers, Mark lifted the girl to the floor although she stood five foot eight and had a buxom, Junoesque build which did not make her a featherweight. Setting her down, Mark gave the girl a kiss she would never forget.

Watching the girl stagger away from Mark looking glassy-eyed, for all her experiences in such matters, Calamity smiled. Yet she made no attempt to leave the bar and go speak words of wisdom to the saloongirl. Not that Calamity was scared of the girl even though slightly smaller and lighter. Nor was the fact that Buffalo Bill, his client and the client's wife sat in the railed-off area reserved for the upper-classes what held Calamity back. At another time Calamity would have gone straight across the room and explained to the girl that although a kiss from Mark Counter was something no female would be likely to forget, nothing would develop from that kiss while Calamity was around. Right now Calamity had something more important to tend to, so she put off pleasure until a later, more convenient time.

The saloon's owner arrived still pulling on his cutaway coat and without a tie around the neck of his unbuttoned shirt. With his swarthily handsome face showing annoyance, Tom Barraclough asked his bartender why the hell he had been called out while working on the business' books.

"That big feller looks like he might be able to lift the weight, boss," was the explanation.

"All right. But why the hell couldn't you handle it without——"

"I thought maybe the politician'd be through talking, seeing how nobody's listening," replied the bartender. "And he don't look like the sort to hang around in a saloon."

With a grunt that might have meant anything, Barraclough turned and studied Mark's giant physique. Like the bartender said, there was a man who looked as if he might be able to do something with the five hundred pound dumb-bell. Most likely he could not lift it clean over his head, nobody had done so yet—even the great Seamus O'Sullivan, for he was no more than a figment of the saloonkeeper's imagination, a come-on which brought much trade to the house. Even should the big cowhand look like succeeding, Barraclough was prepared to prevent him from doing so.

"Go to it, cowhand," Barraclough called. "Let's see you heft that dumb-bell right up there."

Before he started to make the attempt, Mark took certain precautions. He knew the danger to himself should the weight slip while he lifted, so went to the barrel of sawdust standing at the side of the room and helped himself to a double handful. After spreading the sawdust on the bar between the weights, and leaving a film of it on his hands, Mark levered off his boots. High-heeled cowhand boots were ideal for their purpose, but that purpose was not lifting heavy weights and a broken heel could cause Mark a serious injury.

Silence fell on the room as everybody watched Mark approach the dumb-bell. Placing his feet carefully into position, Mark bent, gripped the bar and made sure his hands would not slip. He drew in a couple of deep breaths and then began to lift, spreading his right leg back and bending the left knee. The weight rose slowly from the floor and the crowd watched hardly daring to breathe as the Texan threw all his enormous strength into the task of raising it chest high.

The bartender watched the weight rising as did every other eye in the room, or so he thought. Reaching under the bar, his fingers passed over the ten-gauge shotgun and into a box behind it. The box contained a couple of seemingly innocent objects, yet together they had a sinister and very dangerous purpose. Taking up the boy's bean-shooter from the box, the bartender slipped the shiny pebble which lay beside it into the mouthpiece. He reckoned everybody would be so interested in watching the Texan that none would see him lift the bean-shooter and blow out the pebble.

A click came to the bartender's ears; one sound he recognized any time he heard it for just what it was. Turning his head towards the sound, he looked first into the muzzle of a Navy Colt, then at the cold eyes of Calamity Jane.

"Leave it lie," she ordered in a low voice.

Knowing Calamity, the bartender left it. He did not doubt that she would use the gun if he tried to raise the bean-shooter and blow the pebble at Mark's straining back. Seeing he had not chance now of improving his boss's chances, the bartender rested the flat of his hands on the bartop and watched the big Texan lift the weight.

Mark brought the bar up to chest height, changed his grips, straightened his legs and exerted all his power. A gasp ran through the crowd as the great dumb-bell rose to arms' length above Mark's head and he held it there. For a good five seconds Mark held that great weight over his head. Sweat soaked his body and poured down his naked torso, his muscles bulged and writhed like he had a python under his skin, and his lungs felt they would burst.

At last, in a silence that could almost be felt, Mark started to lower the dumb-bell, letting it swing down, and crash on to the stout timbers before him. For almost twenty seconds nobody moved or breathed loud in the room. Mark staggered slightly and Chaseman sprang to his side, helping him from the oak boards and to a chair at the nearest table.

"Yeeah!" Calamity screamed, firing a shot through the roof of the building.

The shot and yell broke the silence and instantly almost everybody in the room began to shout, cheer, jump up and applaud the blond giant from Texas' mighty effort.

"What happened?" Barraclough snarled, swinging to face his bartender under cover of the excitement following Mark's lifting the dumb-bell.

"Calamity Jane was in the night that bohunk near on

lifted it and guessed why he let it drop. So she had a gun on me and that gal'd shoot a man.''

Barraclough spat out a curse. On a previous occasion when he thought he might lose his money, a pebble blown by the bartender struck the weight-lifter—a bohunk, mid-European worker—causing him to lose his hold. That this crippled the man for life did not concern Barraclough, for it saved his money.

Although the saloonkeeper would willingly have refused to keep his part of the bargain, he knew better than try. The crowd would tear his place, and him, apart should he welch on his deal. So Barraclough forced a sickly smile to his face and walked to where Mark leaned on a table with Calamity Jane and Chaseman at his side.

"Here you are, friend," he said with false joviality, taking out his wallet.

"Forget it," Mark replied. "I don't want the money, but set up the drinks like the notice says."

That was some slight consolation for Barraclough. Anyway, he would make up the money not spent that night from the crowd in the future. Yet it hurt to think of the unprofitable night he was due to have. He could not see any man in the room showing moderation when free drinks could be had for the asking.

"You heard the man," he said, turning to the crowd. "Belly up, it's on the house until midnight."

Barraclough was not the only man who knew what to expect when free drinks were offered. Leaving the bandstand, Thackery made his way across the room and thought unpleasant thoughts about the workers he usually professed such admiration and friendship for.

A man blocked Thackery's path and he looked up to see who it might be, hoping to find some worker who had a greater interest in politics than in free drinks.

"Mr. Thackery," Chaseman said, managing a smile at the man. "Would you come with me, please. I'm afraid I have some bad news for you."

Cold fear hit Thackery at the words. This was his first trip into the wild and untamed West. Always before he campaigned in the East where the police, who he always spoke of in disparaging terms at other times, were on hand to save him from possible danger.

Not having the courage to object, Thackery followed Chaseman across the room. He wondered what the workers would think of his being with the hated boss of the railroad, but need not have worried, none of them showed the slightest interest in anything but getting to the free drinks.

Chaseman led Thackery to where Mark stood by the table putting on his shirt.

"This's Mark Counter, from Texas, Mr. Thackery," Chaseman introduced and nodded to where Calamity Jane stood holding Mark's gunbelt. "And Miss Martha Jane Canary."

"Howdy, Mr. Thackery," Mark said, tucking his shirt into his waistband.

Although Thackery had been away from Texas for many years, and had lost any trace of a Southern accent, he knew that when a cowhand called a man "mister" after being introduced, the cowhand did not like that person.

"Where's your wife to, Mr. Thackery?" Chaseman asked.

A brave man, fearing the evil head of the railroad might have ill-intentions against his wife, might have lied. Thackery was not a brave man.

"D—down at a tent we hired."

Mark finished tucking in his shirt, then took his gunbelt from Calamity. For her part, Calamity eyed the girl Mark had lifted on to the table hopefully. The girl knew Calamity too well to try cutting in on a man whom the red-head had interests in.

"Now Mark's ready we'll go along and see her," Chaseman remarked. "I hope you'll both accept my hospitality for the night. The news we have for you may cause you to need more privacy than a tent could offer."

On leaving the bar, his passing unnoticed by the men he had come so far to sway with his eloquence, Thackery led the men to where his ever-loving wife waited patiently for his return in a mud floored little tent.

Only Marlene Thackery was not patiently waiting. True she was in the tent, but had only just returned to it. Fury swept through her as she tried to comb up her red hair into the neat and tidy style which had been all the rage back east, but proved the very devil to keep neat while traveling, or living in a tent.

A short time ago Marlene had been helping Barra-clough with his book-keeping and his departure, with the warning to get back to her tent, did not please her. She heard her husband's voice outside the tent and made sure the black, stylish traveling dress was buttoned up.

"This is where we're staying," Thackery said. "Are you ready to receive visitors, Marlene?"

"As ready as I could be in this pig-sty," she replied, but under her breath, for it would never do for her to make such a comment about the living accommodation loaned to them by one of the workers.

Expecting to find Thackery had brought a delegation of workers to see her, Marlene lifted the flap of the tent. It came as a pleasant surprise to see a handsome blond giant, a well dressed prosperous looking man with her husband, instead of the usual collection of surly malcontents Thackery, and her father before him, usually brought home to meet her.

All in all, Marlene Thackery was a beautiful, eye-catching woman; Calamity Jane disliked her on sight.

The woman's beauty and eye-catching figure did not cause Calamity's dislike, for Calamity was good looking and shapely enough to stand competition. Nor was it the predatory way in which Marlene eyed Mark; Calamity was not jealous by nature although she would have strenuously opposed anybody cutting in on Mark while at the saloon.

No, Calamity looked beneath the face, reading the cold, arrogant and avaricious nature behind it. To a good-hearted girl like Calamity, Marlene Thackery's type would always be an anathema.

"What did you gentlemen want to see me about?" Thackery asked, getting his confidence back.

He had heard of business men paying unscrupulous members of the Socialist Labor Party handsomely to leave town and wondered if Chaseman intended to make him an offer. Of course he would not throw aside his principles—unless the price should be high enough, for after all, the men at the saloon showed him they were not truly interested in making the world a better place for themselves.

"I'm sorry to have to tell you this," Mark replied. "But your father is dead. Killed in a riding accident."

"And I came to express my condolences and to offer you my hospitality in your grief," Chaseman went on.

"We accept it, sir, thank you," Marlene replied before her husband could open his mouth, for she expected him to refuse; which only showed Marlene did not know Claude Thackery too well.

For a pair of grieving kin-folks, Claude and Marlene Thackery appeared to be bearing up remarkably well. By the time they reached the comfortable visitors' room of Chaseman's private car, they had overcome their grief sufficiently to take an interest in why Mark came to bring them the news.

"Your father asked my boss, Ole Devil Hardin, to gather in the legatees for his will-reading," Mark told the man and woman.

"I hope you've found them all," Thackery replied, although his tone implied he hoped no such thing.

"They'll likely all be in Mulrooney by the end of the week and we'll start for Texas comes Monday."

"May I accommodate you for tonight?" Chaseman asked. "A sleeping berth in one of the cars will offer more privacy than the tent."

"Thank you," Marlene replied, but she kept her eyes on Mark as she spoke. "Could you show us where to go, so we can recover ourselves in privacy?"

"I'll show you," Chaseman promised. "You may as well come and see your berth, Mark."

"Dang buzzards!" Calamity Jane grunted, after the Thackerys disappeared into one of the line of luxurious berths reserved for important visitors to the construction camps. "If they're grieving I'm Wild Bill Hickok, which same I'm not, my hair's too short. What in hell did that gal ever see in him?"

Many people wondered that when they saw the Thackerys. The answer was simple enough. On hearing that Thackery had a very rich father, Marlene married him in the fond hope he would put all the political poverty behind him and return to a life of rich, comfortable leisure. He failed to do so, but Marlene stuck to him—even though she occasionally helped gentlemen like Barraclough with their book-keeping while Thackery made his speeches—and cast her bread hopefully on the waters. Now at last it seemed the tide had come in bearing fancy iced cakes on its waves.

After recovering from their grief, the Thackerys joined Calamity, Chaseman and Mark in the car and sat down to an enjoyable meal. They, the Thackerys, plied Mark with questions about the state of the cattle business in general and Elmo Thackery's part in it in particular, showing a most unSocialistic attitude to the state of the old man's finances.

Finally they prepared to go to their beds, ready to make their departure on the morning train.

"I'll walk you home, Calamity," Mark suggested.

"Why thank you 'most to death," Calamity answered with a grin. "I surely do admire you Southern gentlemen, don't you, Mrs. Thackery?"

Marlene chose to ignore the remark and left on her husband's arm.

Shortly after one o'clock in the morning, Marlene left her bed. Slipping a robe over her nightgown, she threw a glance at her husband as he lay snoring in the other bed. Marlene left the berth and walked along the dimly lit passage to tap gently at another door.

"Mr. Counter," she whispered, hearing bare feet padding across the floor beyond the door. "Mr. Counter?"

"Nope, Miss Canary," replied a feminine voice. "What did you want with Mark?"

"I—er—I wanted to know what time the train leaves."

"Nine-thirty," Calamity replied. "You've plenty of time. Good night."

Turning on her heel, Marlene headed for her bed. She could have sworn that the handsome Texan had been allocated that berth and felt puzzled at her mistake.

CHAPTER FIVE

The Legatees Head South

Elmo Thackery's death brought changes to a number of lives.

Some of the changes showed among the people brought together by Ole Devil Hardin's floating outfit, as they gathered before Freddie Woods' Fair Lady Saloon on Monday morning ready to start their journey to Casa Thackery.

In planning the trip, Dusty Fog hired a covered carriage and a light wagon from Wells Fargo. These would travel faster than a single large covered wagon, carry all the supplies needed for the trip, and offer shelter for the women in inclement weather. On arrival at Casa Thackery, the two vehicles could be returned to the Wells Fargo office in Thackery City.

Francine Thackery looked much improved by the change in living conditions brought about by her grand-father's death. On the first evening after her liberation from Cohen's clutches, Francine had been thoroughly bathed by a couple of sturdy police matrons, then had her hair combed and curled. Good clothes, decent food, and the natural resilience of youth had already thrown aside and driven off her fears and she was forgetting her ill-treatment at Cohen's hands.

If the change in Frankie, as she now liked to be called, was marked, it did not come up to the change in Claude and Marlene Thackery.

Actually the change in Marlene was more mental than physical. She always dressed well, although the ring with a pyramid-shaped cluster of diamonds on her left hand was new. Now her face took on a haughty superiority and her manner became a rich man's wife, or so she thought.

Thackery now wore a Stetson hat, fringed buckskin jacket, white shirt and bow-tie, with levis tucked into riding boots. He might have added a gunbelt, but caution held him from making such a purchase. The Southern accent he had worked so hard to conceal came back to his voice. He, the last living son, would have much to do with the running of the ranch and his dreams of a brave new world for the down-trodden workers had faded the moment he realized he now belonged to the employers-of-labor class.

Almost as marked was the change in Joan Shandley. Her friends would hardly have recognized her had they seen her. She wore a sober, modest black traveling dress and no jewelry, and her face had none of its usual merriment. The death of Beegee Benson hit Joan hard and she was quiet, subdued, ignoring Marlene's hostility and biting comments about her presence in the party.

Although the Ysabel Kid and Waco checked carefully, they could learn nothing about the hired killers. The two killers had been in town for a week, but nobody knew much about them. Nor could any of the Buffalo Hide Saloon staff remember seeing the men inside on the night of the killing. So the reason for the killing remained a mystery. Dusty Fog, on hearing of the incident, made no comment on it, but insisted Joan stayed at the Fair Lady while in Mulrooney and that she and the other legatees were watched all the time by his men.

The idea of the surveillance pleased Marlene at first, but she found her husband suddenly developed an interest in her well-being and never left her side. This had the effect of cramping her style and preventing her making the most of Mark Counter's company. However, she consoled herself with the thought that she ought to have a chance to become better acquainted with the blond giant before they reached Texas, or might even be able to hire him to work on their ranch.

"Let's get ready to roll," Mark called. "Joan, you and Mrs. Thackery share the carriage."

An angry frown creased Marlene's brow. Only the previous evening she had graciously given Mark permission to call her by her Christian name. She did not overlook how he still addressed her as "Mrs." and called that cheap barroom slut "Joan."

"I'll ride the wagon, Mark," Joan said quietly, knowing how things stood between herself and Marlene, and hoping to avoid unpleasantness.

"Can I ride the wagon, too?" Frankie asked, glancing at Waco who sat on the wagon box and shook his head in a negative manner to Mark.

"Sure, go ahead," grinned Mark, who had seen the youngster's head shake. "You take the reins of the carriage, Mr. Thackery."

While it did not fit into Thackery's conception of a rich rancher's duties to drive a carriage, he saw none of the other men intended to do so. Climbing on to the box, he unwrapped the reins and cast an apprehensive eye at the two spirited-looking team horses.

Swinging on to the sidewalk, Mark went to the bat-wing doors of the saloon and looked inside to where Dusty stood talking with Freddie Woods.

"We're ready when you are, Dusty," he said.

"I'll be right out," Dusty replied, then shook Freddie's hand. "We'll have to be moving, Freddie. Telegraph me happen you can make it down to Texas after the trail drive season and I'll not take out on any chores while you're visiting."

"I'll do that," Freddie promised.

Their parting seemed to be rather stilted and formal, but both were satisfied, for they had said their good-byes in a more satisfactory manner earlier and in

privacy. Freddie raised her hand to wave as Dusty went
through the doors and from her sight. Wondering if
there would be an opening for a lady saloonkeeper in
Rio Hondo County, Freddie turned and walked towards
the stairs meaning to catch up on some of the sleep she
had missed over the weekend.

Dusty threw a last look at the saloon before he
mounted his seventeen hand paint stallion. Already
Mark sat astride his equally large bloodbay stud-horse
and had Waco's paint's reins looped around his sad-
dlehorn. The Kid lounged to one side afork his magnificent white stallion, an animal that looked even wilder
and more dangerous than its master. Half a dozen spare
team horses were roped to the rear of the wagon. All
appeared to be as Dusty ordered it to be the previous
night.

"Let 'em roll!" he ordered.

After the first few worrying moments Thackery found
he could handle the carriage horses, and soon had
himself convinced that he drove them because he was
the best man for the job. On the wagon's box Joan
smiled a little as she watched Frankie's attempts to
attract Waco's attention and the young cowhand's
equally determined efforts to avoid the girl's juvenile
infatuation.

Once clear of town, and pointing south along much
the same route as the OD Connected herd drove north,
the Kid swung his horse from the rest of the party and
found a knoll from which he could watch their back-
trail. If Beegee Benson's death had been caused by
mistaken identity, there might be other attempts to kill
Joan. The attempts could also be aimed at the other
legatees; for that appeared to be the most likely motive
for anybody wanting Joan Shandley dead. Dusty Fog
did not believe in taking unnecessary risks when they
could be avoided by forethought.

It appeared Dusty's precautions were not needed.
When the Kid joined the others as they made camp for

the night, he told them nobody appeared to be following them. Although the day's travel had been uneventful, the night saw a clash of wills between Marlene and Joan.

On halting the party Dusty gave his orders for making camp. Mark and Thackery were to help him tend to the horses. Seeing how Waco tried to avoid Frankie's girlish attentions, Dusty grinned and told him to help the youngster gather buffalo chips as fuel for the fire. Joan volunteered to act as cook for the trip, an offer Dusty accepted. This left Marlene unemployed. Her attitude indicated she considered a rich rancher's wife—like her husband, Marlene now regarded herself as being one of the rangeland aristocracy—should not be expected to demean herself by doing common work.

Joan failed to subscribe to the idea. Maybe she might not have worried with a different woman, but she remembered Marlene's sneers and veiled insinuations about her relationship with Elmo Thackery. Whatever the reason, Joan intended to see Marlene did her share of the work, so asked the other woman to lend her a hand.

"Me?" gasped Marlene.

"You!" Joan replied with just as much emphasis on the one word.

"I can't cook," Marlene answered in a tone which implied, cooking would be beneath her dignity.

"You can help peel vegetables and wash dishes," Joan snapped back.

A gurgle of merriment left Frankie's lips, for she had been close enough to hear the words. Seeing her aunt turn an angry face in her direction, Frankie scuttled off after Waco. She hoped Aunt Marlene would be made to work, for the little she had seen of her newly met relative did not make Frankie like the woman, but she did like Joan.

"I, wash dishes?" gasped Marlene.

"You've probably done it before."

"How dare you speak to me like that?" Marlene asked, her voice rising. "I—Claude——!"

"Your husband's not handling this outfit!" Joan answered, her temper rising. "Cap'n Fog's the one to see."

Marlene swung towards Dusty, sure her beauty, charm and the fact that she was the wife of a rich rancher would sway his decision in a way favorable to her. Much to her annoyance none of the three attributes appeared to have any effect on the small Texan.

"B-but my husband——" Marlene began when told to help Joan.

"Is helping Mark with the horses," Dusty interrupted. "We've a long ride ahead of us, Mrs. Thackery. I asked your husband if he wanted to hire a cook and drivers, he said not and told me we could manage. That 'we' means all of us have to do our share."

A furious Marlene went to work cursing, under her breath, her husband's greed. He could have hired men to do the work, but he did not see why he should waste money; particularly his own money for the hiring would be paid for by his father's estate.

After the first couple of days the party settled down into a smooth routine, with the women handling the cooking and the men tending to the horses. Nothing disturbed their even flowing routine, the Kid rode scout but saw no sign of danger.

Marlene's hatred of Joan grew daily, for Joan was getting over her shock and grief to become her usual friendly, merry self. After repeated failures to become better acquainted with Mark, Marlene tried her charms on Dusty, followed by the Kid and as a last resort attempted to draw Waco into her net. All her attempts failed and the sight of Joan laughing, talking and making herself agreeable to the cowhands made Marlene hate the little saloongirl all the more. Despite all Marlene thought, Joan's friendship with the cowhands was harmless and platonic. Joan was warm and friendly by nature and her years as a saloon hostess gave her the ability to be sociable and friendly with men without letting it go further.

Proof of Dusty's wisdom in selecting the light wagon and carriage to transport the women showed in the good time they made going south. Having left Kansas and crossed half of Oklahoma Territory, Dusty felt they might be out of danger. He did not relax his precautions and the Kid still rode scout.

The camp had been set up one evening when the Kid rode in through the gathering darkness. Leaving his big white stallion standing like a statue even though free, the Kid walked to where Dusty stood taking his bedroll from the wagon.

"We've got company, Dusty," he said.

"Who?"

"Ten or a dozen of them. Been on our trail all day."

"Huh huh!" grunted Dusty. "Reckon they're cowhands on their way home?"

"They're sticking to our tracks," the Kid replied. "Even swung west along that stream we crossed, like we did, only they don't have wagons along."

Both pieces of information had significance when taken together. Earlier in the day Dusty's party swung west for a mile following the banks of a small river until finding a ford suitable for taking the wagons across. Men on horseback and without wagons could have swum the river and saved time in making a detour. If the men were cowhands heading home to Texas after a trail drive, they might have followed the wagons in the hope of receiving a free meal that evening. Yet this following party had not come to Dusty's camp. Dusty did not like the implication behind the Kid's words.

"And they're not coming in?" Dusty asked.

"Nope. Settled down in a hollow as soon as it started to get dusk. Could see our fire in the distance too."

Which meant the men had not followed them in the hope of receiving a free meal. Dusty thought quickly, remembering something the marshal of Mulrooney told him about a new style of robbery being practiced around the trail drive routes.

Since the death of Jethro Kliddoe at Dusty's hands,* and the breaking up of his gang, the stopping of trail herds and demanding head tax toll—on threat of having the herd stampeded—had died out. Now the border scum tried to catch the trail bosses heading home with the money from the sale of their cattle. Dusty had sold his herd and carried the proceeds of the sale in his saddlebags, a sum of money sufficient to tempt a gang of outlaws despite the reputations of the men carrying it.

"Go look them over, Lon," Dusty ordered.

"Sure," agreed the Kid.

"Come and get it! Come and get it before I throw it to the hogs!" Frankie yelled from the fire, where she had been helping Joan prepare supper.

"That lil gal's sure come out of herself," grinned the Kid. "I'll eat before I ride, Dusty."

"Sure. There'll be nothing moving yet awhiles."

After eating his meal, the Kid went to his horse, mounted and rode off into the darkness. While his departure meant nothing to Joan, Frankie and the Thackerys it caused Waco and Mark to exchange glances, then head towards Dusty.

"What's wrong, Dusty?" Mark asked.

"Lon saw a bunch dogging us all day. He's just rode out to look them over."

"You expecting trouble?" Waco put in eagerly.

"Maybe, boy. You and Mark keep your eyes and ears open."

The party did not sit up late after supper any night and this proved to be no exception. After the women washed the dishes and cleaned up the camp, they went to their beds. The Thackerys slept in the wagon; Joan and Frankie, being small enough to sleep in comfort,

---

* Told in *Trail Boss* by J. T. Edson.

used the carriage seats for their beds; the Texans mostly spread their bedrolls around the fire.

"I've got a feeling we're being watched, Dusty," Waco said as he closed the hook and eye fasteners of the tarp around his bedroll.

"We are," agreed Dusty.

"Sure," drawled Mark, eyeing the youngster tolerantly. "You've been so busy sparking Frankie you never heard a horse grunt down the trail."

"Sparking!" Waco yelped indignantly. "That danged fool button spends near on all her waking hours chasing me."

"It's what Cousin Betty calls the fascination of the horrible, boy," grinned Dusty.

"And she should ought to know," Waco answered. "She's got some horrible kin. Present company not necessarily excepted."

"Go talk to your gal," Mark ordered. "How about that feller out there, Dusty?"

"Leave him be. Lon'll find him on his way back and handle things without disturbing the womenfolk."

"Hey!" Joan yelled from the carriage. "Don't you bunch sit talking all the night. There's some of us need our beauty sleep."

"Yes, ma'am," Dusty answered. "There sure is."

For a moment there was silence. Then Joan caught Dusty's meaning and her reply came blunt and pungent, although not entirely to the point. Then, chuckling to herself, Joan drew up the blankets and prepared to sleep.

Time dragged by and to all intents and purposes the camp lay sleeping.

"He's still out there," Waco said, without lifting his head from his saddle "pillow". "That's a noisy hoss he's got."

"Sure," Dusty agreed in no louder tones.

At that moment the Kid returned, coming from the opposite direction to the one taken on his departure. He acted in a casual manner, tending to his horse and helping himself to a cup of coffee from the pot on the fire, then feeding logs on the fire before going to where Mark had spread his bedroll.

"They're after us for sure, Dusty," he said quietly, speaking to the apparently sleeping shapes. "Got a man out that ways watching the camp and aim to come in on us around midnight when we're all fast asleep."

"They tell you all that?" asked Waco.

"You might say that, boy. I was thereabouts when they fixed it. Only I was closer to them than their man is to us."

Knowing the shadow-silent way the Kid could move and his almost uncanny ability to hide behind the smallest cover, the other men showed no surprise at his words.

"You doing anything about the feller who's watching us?" Mark asked.

"Nope. I figgered to let him go back and tell his bunch we're all hard to sleeping. If they're going to hit us, let's get it over and done with tonight."

"I'll go along with you, Lon," Dusty drawled.

"He's moving off now," the Kid said. "Walks soft, must have some Injun blood in his veins."

"Happen he comes back we'll let some of it out again," Waco promised.

None of the others heard a sound, but relied on the Kid's keen ears not to steer them wrong. For five minutes they lay as if sleeping, with the Kid preparing his bed. Then he gave a grunt of annoyance and rose from where he had been sitting on his bedroll.

"I'll just wander around and make sure there's only the one and that he's far gone," he said in a low voice, then spoke louder and in more carrying tones. "Danged if I don't have to go!"

"Well go and make less noise!" Frankie called from the carriage and then giggled at her nerve.

"Never could stand giggling gals," growled Waco.

"Not unless they was a few years older than her."

Silence fell on the camp and for fifteen minutes nothing happened. Then the Ysabel Kid returned and headed straight towards the other cowhands.

"They only had the one man out there," he said. "He's gone back to tell the others we're all safe and sleeping."

"Reckon we'd best make sure they find us that way then," Dusty replied.

Some instinct kept nagging at the leader of the outlaw bunch as they moved silently towards the sleeping camp. He could not think what was worrying him, but he felt vaguely perturbed.

Apparently the camp's occupants were sleeping heavily, for the fire had been allowed to die down to glowing embers. Their horses appeared to have strayed, but this would be an advantage for the further from the shooting the horses were, the less chance of them stampeding.

He shook off the nagging doubts and waved his men forward, sending each one dashing to the place allocated to him when they laid their plans. Two men went to the rear of the wagon and fired shots into the shapes on the floor. Another pair reached the carriage at the same moment, tearing open a door to throw lead into the dark interior. The remaining men shot at the shapes by the fire, sending bullets into them. The silence of the night shattered by exploding powder and lit to the winking flare of revolvers' muzzle blasts.

"There's something wrong!" one of the men yelled.

The same thought struck the others at about the same time. Sure their attack had been swift and silent, but they knew at least one of their victims ought to be making either sound or movement.

"Drop the guns and raise your hands!" a voice called from the darkness beyond the camp.

"It's a trap!" yelled one of the gang, throwing a shot

at where he thought the voice originated.

From four points around the camp flame lanced out, three Winchester rifle shots and the light crack of a Winchester carbine ringing out. Two of the gang slid down in the limp manner of head-shot men. A third man clutched his leg, gave a scream of pain and collapsed. Although a fourth took a bullet, he kept his feet and joined the remainder in a panic-stricken flight from the death trap into which they rushed in search of loot.

"Take after them, Lon, Waco!" Dusty ordered. "Make sure they won't be coming back. Mark, go see to the women."

"Yo!" came Mark's cavalry-inspired reply.

The Kid and Waco had their horses with them, saddled ready for use and the sound of their departing hooves came to Dusty's ears as he walked towards the camp. Carbine in hand, Dusty advanced to where the wounded man tried to rise but failed when his bullet-broken leg collapsed under him.

"D-don't shoot, mister!" the man yelled. "I'm done."

"You never said a truer word," Dusty replied. "Move clear of that gun."

"I got a busted leg!" whined the man.

"You'll have a busted head to match it happen you don't move!" Dusty snapped back and the man moved painfully away from the revolver he had dropped when hit.

"Who're you bunch?" Dusty went on, moving closer.

For a moment the man did not reply. He studied Dusty, noting the easy familiarity with which the small Texan handled his Winchester '73 carbine. Nor did the way in which Dusty moved go unnoticed by the man. Small the Texan might be, but he handled himself like a trained lawman.

"We rode for Tom Klay, that's him there by the

fire," the raider finally said. "My leg hurts like hell, mister."

"I'll tend to it—after you've done some talking."

A flurry of shots sounded not too far away, followed by a wild, savage, nerve-tingling Comanche scalp yell, that made the man look around nervously, and the ringing "yeeah!" of the Confederate cavalry. Then the man heard hooves fading off into the distance and knew his companions had deserted him to his fate.

"Why'd you come after us?" asked Dusty.

"F-for the cattle money you got."

"How'd you know about it?"

Again the man hesitated before answering and looked to where he could hear the sound of approaching horses and a pleasant tenor voice lifted in song:

> "In Mobile, in Mobile,
> The eagles they fly high in Mobile,
> Man, the eagles fly so high,
> And they'll drop it in your eye,
> It's lucky cows don't fly in Mobile."

"That's the Ysabel Kid coming," Dusty warned and saw the man knew his dark young friend's name. "You can talk easy for me, or you will talk for him."

"I told you all I know, mister, honest!" yelped the raider. "Klay had been scouting in Mulrooney and come in a couple of days back to say you and your bunch was coming."

"Then why'd you throw lead into the wagon and carriage?" Dusty asked.

"That was Klay's idea. He scouted your camp, said you'd got two guys with rifles in each and that we should burn them before they took to fogging down on us."

CHAPTER SIX

Thackery's Will

The wounded raider stuck to his story even in the face of threats of a prolonged and painful interview at the hands of the Ysabel Kid. In view of the man's fear and the pain of his wound, it seemed likely he told the truth when he claimed his boss brought word of a trail boss heading for Texas with his cattle-sale money. The only significant point to emerge from the questioning was that Klay did not usually handle the scouting of his victims, but had done so on this occasion.

Dusty let the matter rest for a time. The Kid and Waco had come up to the remainder of the gang, killing one and wounding another before the rest scattered and fled. After doing what they could for the prisoner, Dusty, Waco and the Kid removed the bodies and allowed Mark to bring Thackery and the women back to the camp. The following morning the party moved on, calling in at Bent's Ford to hand the wounded raider over to Duke Bent. Dusty sent a telegraph message to the town marshal in Mulrooney asking for information about Tom Klay, raider, in the hope of learning something about the man's activities in town.

Nothing more of note happened for the remainder of the trip. The party made good time and towards noon one day came in sight of the stately old house which formed the hub of Thackery's great Leaning T outfit.

Casa Thackery had been built to withstand enemy

attacks, the weather and the ravages of time. It stood out in the center of rolling prairie land and looked for all the world like an Old Mexico *hacienda*. The same brains which designed and built the great houses below the border had been responsible for erecting the fine old two storey house long before it came into Thackery's hands.

The house, its out-buildings and the wall surrounding them all had been built out of stone in the days when labor was so cheap that mighty structures could be erected for a fraction of what they would cost in the present day. For all his meanness, Elmo Thackery never allowed the maintenance of his home to lapse.

Three people stood on the steps leading to the main doors of the house, a fourth, a tall, black dressed man, behind them. All watched the approaching party with interest. As he rode through the gates, leading the party in, Dusty wondered if one of the quarter might have some guilty knowledge. On second thoughts Dusty absolved the man at the rear, for he knew Frank Gaunt very well.

Mamie Thackery made the first move, coming down the steps towards the party as they brought their horses to a halt before the house. Never had two people been less alike in every way than Mamie and Elmo Thackery. She was short, plump, in her early fifties, although her dark hair did not show it, and her merry, friendly face had a love of life to it. Despite all the years spent with him, the woman showed nothing of her brother's suspicious, mean nature.

"Hello, Claude," Mamie greeted, without any great enthusiasm, then her face softened and she advanced to place her hands on Frankie's shoulders. "You must be Francine."

The gentleness of Mamie's tones brought Frankie into her arms and the girl kissed her, then turned to Joan who Mark Counter had just helped from the wagon.

"This is Joan, she's my friend," Frankie said, and

Joan could not have come to Mamie Thackery with a better recommendation.

"Hello, Dustine," Jennie Thackery said, coming down the steps after her aunt and making straight for the small Texan.

"Hello, Jennie," Dusty replied. "Come and meet your kin."

This was the girl Elmo Thackery tried to persuade Ole Devil Hardin would make a good wife for Dusty; and also link the two families' fortunes together. She stood about an inch taller than Dusty, slim, pallid, beautiful, with shoulder-long red hair. There was a hint of Elmo's nature about Jennie, a coldness which would have chilled Dusty even if his uncle had considered Thackery's offer worthwhile. Like her aunt, Jennie wore black mourning clothes and the dress did nothing to make her attractive, for she must be the one person who genuinely grieved over her grandfather's death. In fact Jennie had been the only living person Thackery cared for. Only Jennie's presence caused Thackery to keep his home in the luxurious manner it showed.

"Dusty looks as keen to meet that gal as I was to have young Frankie straddle me," Waco whispered to Mark.

"It's a mite more serious than that," Mark answered *sotto voce*. "Say, just look at Thackery, will you."

For a moment after stepping down from the carriage, ignoring his wife who was still inside, Claude Thackery looked at his home. His eyes turned to where the tall, darkly handsome Vint Borg, clad in a black mourning outfit instead of his range clothes, came towards him. Thackery's main memories of young Vint Borg covered several thrashings and numerous practical jokes at the hands of the cowhand who was now foreman, and whose father's loyalty helped found the Thackery fortune.

On his way south Thackery had thought out a pompous welcome speech to be delivered to his foreman; covering lightly Thackery's satisfaction with the way the spread had been run, hinting that improvement must be

made, and that Borg's selfless devotion to the master of
the house would be expected and might bring its own
reward at a later date.

Somehow the words would not come and the old
feeling of inadequacy returned as he faced Borg.

"Howdy, Claude," Borg said with easy familiarity,
throwing a glance towards the carriage and stepping forward to hand Marlene down. "And you must be good
ole Claude's missus. Man, Claude, I never thought
you'd got such good taste. My name's *Vint* Borg,
ma'am, and when we're better acquainted, why I'll tell
you things you never knowed about Claude."

"I can hardly wait, Vint," Marlene replied, holding
his hand longer than her watching husband thought
necessary. "And of course any friend of Claude must
call me Marlene."

Although Thackery thought of stating an employee
could hardly be classed as a friend and should not be on
first-name terms with his employer, he did not speak.
His silence was due to Lawyer Gaunt moving forward;
and the fact that he doubted whether Borg would accept
his comments as became a hired man. That lousy
Socialist Labor bunch were ruining the workers, making
them lose all their respect for their betters.

"Ladies and gentlemen," Gaunt said, interrupting
the greetings and talk. "I'm sorry to butt in like this,
but I wish to read the will."

Any thoughts of speech-making, or objections to the
hired help's attitude, left Thackery, being replaced by a
desire to know how much of his father's worldly goods
would be coming his way.

"I think the library would be the best place," he said,
in the manner of the owner granting a favor. "Come,
Marlene."

"Dustine," Mamie put in, "I'd like you along."

"Sure, Aunt Mamie. Where can the boys put up their
horses?"

"In the stables, the harness stock can go in the corral.

I've arranged for rooms to be made ready. We're a bit crowded, but I've four beds in one of the larger rooms that you and your boys can use."

Throwing an angry glare at his aunt's back, Thackery tried to send her a telepathic order to put the OD Connected men in the bunkhouse with the Thackery hands, if they had to be encouraged to stay on eating his food. His effort failed to have any result, for Mamie called to a Mexican servant who had been waiting in the hall and gave orders to show the cowhands to the stables, then on to their quarters in the main house.

The legatees, Dusty and Gaunt made their way across the entrance hall and into the library which had been prepared hurriedly on the party being seen in the distance. A half circle of chairs faced a long, polished oak table in the center of the room. Lawyer Gaunt walked around the table and stood with his back to the fireplace over which hung a portrait of Thackery, Ole Devil Hardin, James Bowie and Sam Houston dressed in their Mexican War uniforms and looking dashing young blades. Dusty knew the portrait well, its original hung over the fireplace in his uncle's gun-decorated library. Not that Dusty had much time to study the portrait for Gaunt got down to business as soon as the others took their seats.

Taking a long envelope from the inside pocket of his coat, Gaunt handed it across the table saying, "Would you examine the seal on this document, Captain Fog?"

"Sure," Dusty replied, accepting the envelope and studying the blob of red wax on the sealed-down flap. It bore the Leaning T mark which Thackery used as a brand and appeared to have been made with the signet ring Thackery always wore. "I'd say it was intact and untouched."

"Thank you," Gaunt answered. "Would you pass the envelope to anybody who wishes to examine it?"

Without waiting to be asked, Dusty passed the envelope to Thackery, who took it and studied it as if he knew what he was doing. After a careful scrutiny Thackery handed the envelope to Gaunt, his whole attitude indicating further examination would be unnecessary now he had decided the seal was all right.

None of the others spoke, but Dusty saw Borg grin and wink at Marlene who smiled in return. Happen Thackery did not watch his step, he would have trouble with his wife and foreman. Turning his head, Dusty glanced at the others, all showed some interest in the proceedings. Jennie sat rigid in her seat, her pallid face stiff with expectancy although she darted glances at the other members of the gathering as if wondering why they had been brought to her home.

"This is the last will and testament of Elmo Thackery," Gaunt told the others. "I will dispense with the legal formalities and get straight down to his wishes for the disposal of his fortune if this meets with your approval."

"Carry on," Thackery answered without consulting any of the others.

"Thank you," Gaunt replied dryly. "The will says I, Elmo Thackery, leave my entire property and wealth to be divided equally——"

"Divided equally!" Thackery barked, looking at the other people in the room, with particular emphasis on Joan Shandley and Vint Borg.

"To be divided equally," Gaunt repeated in a cold tone, "between my sister Mamie, who helped keep my house in order for many years; my granddaughter Jennie, whose love and affection served as a crutch in my declining years; my son Peter, or his heirs should he be passed away; my son Claude, who never came near me; his wife Marlene, who I never saw; Vinton Borg, whose father helped found my fortune; and lastly Joan Shandley, who kindly bought an old man a meal when she believed him to be down on his luck."

"And she gets an equal share——!" began Thackery.

"Shut up, listen and don't be a hog, Claude!" Mamie snapped.

"Thank you, Mamie," Gaunt said and looked down at the paper. "There is a clause to the will which reads: The entire fortune will be shared out three months from the date of my death among the seven people listed. If any one of them should not be in Casa Thackery at that time for any reason, that one's share will be divided among the remainder."

"Does that mean what I think it means?" Dusty asked quietly.

"What do you think it means, Captain Fog?" Gaunt replied.

"That if all but one of these people died, the entire fortune would pass to that one."

Even as he spoke Dusty could not shake off the feeling that he was being watched. Yet none of the legatees had given him as much as a glance while listening to the will being read.

"That's just what it means, Captain," Gaunt answered. "Although in the case of Marlene and Claude Thackery, as man and wife with equal property rights, if one should die the other would have a good claim to the one's share, which might not be legal terminology, but explains what I mean the more clearly."

"Would the will stand up legally?" Dusty went on.

"It would, despite its unusual conditions. Elmo Thackery was in sound mind and body when he made it. Why do you ask?"

"Reckon I was just curious," Dusty drawled and settled back in his seat.

Gaunt gave the small Texan a long, searching look. One thing the lawyer knew for sure, Dusty did not ask questions out of idle curiosity. However, a glance around the room, then at Dusty's face told Gaunt it would be a waste of time to take the matter further.

"Does my father say anything about m—who will run

the ranch until the three months are up?" Thackery asked.

"How do you mean, run it?" growled Borg. "I reckon I ran it all right for the past two years."

"I'm sure Vint has the experience and ability to handle things for us," Marlene put in. "After all, darling, you're not exactly a rancher."

"I'm trustee to the estate," Gaunt said, before Thackery could make any comment on his ability to handle the matter. "Vint will carry on as foreman and I am allowed to grant the payment of two hundred and fifty dollars a month to each of you against the estate, as well as to authorize any other payments of money that I feel may be necessary."

This idea did not please Claude Thackery, but he could think of no valid objections. He thought of contesting the will in court, and wished he had spent more time at his legal studies and less on protest marching or other political activities. Had he done so, he would now possess a clearer idea of his chances of successfully contesting the will and grabbing the lion's share of his father's fortune.

"Are there any other questions?" asked Gaunt.

"Sure," Borg replied, taking his eyes from Marlene. "How much do we get?"

"I haven't the exact figures on hand," the lawyer answered. "But I'd say in the region of two hundred and fifty thousand dollars—each."

Talk welled up, low but intense among the group of people for none of them had realized such an enormous sum would be involved.

"As much as that?" Dusty said quietly when the talk died down.

"As much as that," agreed Gaunt. "Now, if there is nothing more for us to discuss I would suggest we let our new arrivals retire to their rooms to rest and tidy up before dinner."

After the others left the room, Dusty caught the

lawyer's arm and suggested they had a talk in private. Without asking any questions, Gaunt agreed. The lawyer escorted Dusty upstairs and along a passage to the largest of the guest rooms. All the others of the party shared the same passage, despite Thackery's hints that he and his wife should be given the best quarters in the house.

Dusty's three *amigos* had not yet arrived from tending the horses, giving the small Texan a chance to talk privately with Gaunt. This did not imply a lack of trust in his friends, Dusty knew Gaunt would not wish to discuss private and confidential matters before too many witnesses.

Although the room's large double bed had been replaced with four smaller to be used by the Texans, the other furnishings remained. In addition to the big wardrobe, dressing table and washstand, there was a large, built-in cupboard. Dusty took advantage of being first into the room to select the softest bed. Dropping his hat and gunbelt on the bed, Dusty sat down and told the lawyer to take a seat.

"What's worrying you, Dusty?" Gaunt asked, dropping the formal "Captain."

"The same that's worrying you. Thackery's will."

"I didn't like the idea of it from the beginning," the lawyer admitted. "I told Thackery his terms would be an open invitation to somebody to try and get rid of the other beneficiaries."

"What did he say to that?"

"Just laughed that mean laugh of his. Said nobody would be fool enough to try it as the last alive must be the one who killed the rest."

"So they would," agreed Dusty. "But one or two out of the way raises the take for everybody and spreads out the suspicion, if it was cleverly done."

Taking out his cigar case, Gaunt opened it and offered Dusty a thick, black cigar.

"Not for me, I only smoke tobacco," grinned Dusty.

"I got these from your Uncle Devil," replied the lawyer.

"Yeah, I thought so. They're some he had sent as a Christmas present. I wondered how he'd get rid of them," Dusty drawled, then became more serious. "How many people knew the conditions of Thackery's will?"

"Only two. Thackery and myself."

"Tell me all about it," Dusty suggested. "All I know was what the telegraph message Uncle Devil sent me said."

Quickly and concisely Gaunt went into the full story of Thackery's will and the preparations made for the old man's death. Dusty sat on the bed and took one of his matched Colts from its holster. While listening to the lawyer, Dusty began to spin and twirl the gun in a flashing circle upon his trigger finger. It said much for the lawyer's powers of concentration that he could tell his story without a mistake while watching one of the finest exhibitions of gun juggling it had ever been his privilege to see.

"So only you and Thackery knew about the will and that he had traced his other heir and heiresses?" Dusty asked, flipping the Colt into the air and catching it as it fell.

"That's correct."

"Not even Jennie knew?"

"She says not," replied Gaunt. "I may say that surprised me. She knew more about Elmo's actions than any other living soul. Yet she claimed she hadn't heard a thing."

"Could anybody have gotten hold of the will and read it?" Dusty went on.

"No. I came out here on Elmo's request, made out the will with just himself and I in the library. He called in two of his Mexican house servants, who probably can't read English and anyway didn't get a chance as the will was covered over except for the part on which they made their marks as witnesses. Thackery sent them out of the room before he sealed the will in an envelope, using his signet ring to mark it. You yourself examined the seal and saw it to be intact. And the sealed envelope has been locked in Thackery's deed box, fastened in my safe, ever since."

"Which means it couldn't have been known about," Dusty said quietly.

"What's all this about, Dusty?" asked Gaunt. "And don't say you're only curious, because I won't believe you."

"I'm curious all right. Somebody tried to kill Joan Shandley."

Not by a flicker of his face did Gaunt show any surprise at the words, but he sat a little straighter on the bed and watched Dusty's face the closer.

"When?" asked the lawyer.

"In Newton. The night Lon and Waco arrived to tell her the news," Dusty replied and told Gaunt what happened.

"They could have been after the Benson girl."

"Sure, Frank, but I don't buy that. Then there was another hit, this time at all of us."

This time Gaunt did show some surprise. He let the cigar fall from his hand and on to the bed. Catching it up hurriedly, Gaunt dusted the ash off the blankets. He made no comment as Dusty told the story of the attack in Oklahoma. Once more the lawyer raised an objection.

"That game's been done before, raiding a trail boss on his way home."

"Sure," Dusty admitted. "But there were parts of it I didn't like. I reckon the boys and I are well enough known for a raiding party to think twice before they came after us. Yet this bunch did it, and they hit the wagons, would have killed all four legatees had they been inside. It still could've been a precaution—except that their boss had seen the women and Thackery go to bed and knew where they'd be. He didn't usually do his own scouting, but he did that time."

"Why?"

"Two reasons: first, to make sure where the folks he wanted dead were——"

"And the second?"

"To stop his men knowing they were gunning down women until it was too late to avoid it."

"But that implies previous knowledge," Gaunt objected. "And only two people had access to that knowledge."

"Only one, Frank."

"What do you mean?" snapped Gaunt.

"Thackery was dead, only you knew," Dusty answered with a smile. "It'd look bad for you, if those attempts came off."

"Don't say that, Dusty!" growled the lawyer. "Don't even say it as a joke."

"It was in poor taste," Dusty replied. "I'm sorry, Frank. But what I said could sound that way to the law."

"I know it could, Lord, I hated the thought of this business from the start, and it's not getting better."

"Sure," Dusty agreed. "I wasn't too happy about getting involved in it myself and I'm getting less happy all the time."

CHAPTER SEVEN

Frankie's Unpleasant Bedfellow

Although dinner at Casa Thackery had never been a lively meal, the coming of the OD Connected men brought a change to the atmosphere. It might almost seem that the death of Elmo Thackery had lifted a cloud of gloom which lay on the house, for the room seemed brighter, the food more pleasant and conversation bounced around in a manner that had never happened while the rancher lived.

Sitting at one end of the long table, Mamie Thackery looked around the big dining room, which also served as a sitting room and had comfortable chairs, a couple of divans and a grand piano. Only very rarely did more than three people use the room; now, with extra lights and the best table-service, the room glowed with the kind of life that must have filled it in the days of the Spanish ownership.

Claude Thackery, who occupied the seat at the other end of the table, had come in with the determination to impose the full majesty of his person on the others. He found Aunt Mamie had already told the others she would not mind laughter and talk, nor regard it as an affront to her dead brother's memory. For the first time Claude realized that he did not own Casa Thackery, but only had a share in the place. Even his wife, who wore her most daring evening gown, seemed to have voted for an entertaining evening instead of one of boredom.

"Say, does anybody play that fancy piano?" asked Mark when the meal ended and the table was cleared.

"Jennie can," Mamie answered doubtfully. "Will you, dear?"

"Go on, Jennie, please," Frankie put in.

The two girls had seen little of each other and Frankie wondered if Jennie was avoiding her for some reason. So Frankie hoped asking to hear Jennie play the piano would make her cousin become more friendly.

Throwing a glance at Dusty, Jennie crossed to the piano and raised its lid. Sitting down, she began to play the sort of music her grandfather had liked. Although she played well, Jennie was not playing the kind of music the people around the table wished to hear. They applauded her when she finished playing, but none of them wished her to play an encore. Sensing this, Jennie rose and left the piano.

"I've never played one this fancy," Joan remarked, crossing to the piano and running a forefinger along the keyboard. "But I'll give her a whirl if I can."

"Go ahead, Joan gal," Borg answered, for he was dining with the family instead of among the cowhands. "You're one of the owners now."

A slightly embarassed silence followed the words. Dusty looked at Borg with cold eyes. He did not know how good a foreman the other might be, but he sure could not take his liquor. Borg seemed to have been celebrating his good fortune, for he appeared to have been carrying a fair load of coffin-varnish when he came in to dinner and made good use of the wine bottles through the meal.

For a moment none of the others spoke, then Mamie, throwing a look which ought to have chilled Borg, rose and walked towards Joan. The little saloongirl stood erect, eyes going to the faces at the table. On one only, Marlene's, did she read mocking contempt, Borg leered at her with a slobbering lipped grin, Thackery eyed her in a manner she knew all too well, Jennie's face remained an impassive mask, the others showed their annoyance at her embarrassment.

"How about it, Joan?" Mamie asked. "Do you reckon you could play *Ole Dan Tucker* for us?"

The friendly words seemed to break the tension, though not the hate and hostility on Marlene's face. Sitting at the piano, Joan reached for the keys.

"I can try."

"Hold it," Mark called. "Let's heft back the table and twirl the ladies."

"Go ahead," Mamie answered. "I'll get the servants, it takes half a dozen of them to move it."

"We don't need them," grinned Mark. "Let's tote her back, boys."

Eager hands lifted the heavy table and moved it to one side, putting it against the wall. Mamie, with Frankie's help, moved back the carpets to leave a dance floor as large as in many a saloon and plenty large enough even for cowhand-style dancing.

"Let her rip, Joan!" Mamie called.

With deft touch, though not always hitting quite the right note, Joan began to beat out the rollicking rhythm of *Ole Dan Tucker*. While Joan had played on a number of saloon pianos, none had been as classy an instrument as the one she now sat at. A smile came to her face as she hit a sour note, for she decided she could always lay the blame on the piano sounding so good.

"My pleasure, ma'am," Mark said, walking across the room to where Mamie and Marlene stood talking.

Marlene's smile died away, for the tall Texan held out his hand to Mamie and led the old woman gallantly on to the floor. Nor was Marlene's temper improved when she saw the Kid escort Jennie out and Waco take Frankie, although it appeared that Frankie did all the taking.

"How's about you 'n' me twirling a few, Marlene?" Borg asked, lurching up to the woman and scooping her into his arms before she could answer.

At another time Marlene might have enjoyed dancing, but Borg breathed wine and whisky fumes into her face and danced cowhand style; a dance fashion which had little grace or regard for the music in it.

At last Joan brought the tune's beat to an end and received both applause and requests to play some more. Lawyer Gaunt stepped from where he had been standing with Dusty by the punchbowl on the side-piece and walked towards the piano.

"Let me take the stool, Joan," he suggested. "We need some more lady partners to share out."

"I'll wear me a heifer brand, if you like," Waco called from where Frankie clung on to his arm and plied him with eager questions.

"What's that?" she asked.

Mark explained. "Lot of times out here at a dance, there's not enough girls to go around. So some of the fellers have a white rag tied round their arms and that makes 'em gals for the night. We call it wearing a heifer brand."

"Sure, and the feller wearing one gets to sit with the ladies all night," the Kid went on.

The explanation left Frankie with an interesting choice. Either she could have Waco as a partner, or, if he wore the heifer brand, she was able to sit with him between dances.

"If I play the piano we shouldn't need it," Gaunt grinned, having heard how things stood between Waco and the girl and wanting to join in the fun.

"Lay to it, colonel," grinned the Kid, slapping his shirt pocket. "Dang my hide, I've left my makings."

"So have we," chorused Mark, Dusty and Waco, who knew their friend's absent-mindedness where tobacco and papers were concerned.

"I'll go up and get them," he grinned. "My grand-pappy allus told me pale-faces was mean."

"But how about me?" Jennie put in a trifle too

quickly. "I'll be left without a partner. You know Dustine doesn't care for dancing."

"Why, ma'am," answered the Kid with a flourish, "I could never refuse a beautiful lady."

"Nor me," Borg said. "Especially when she's rich."

Luckily the music started up and Mark's hand fell on the Kid's sleeve. With a cold look and unspoken promise to have words with Vint Borg at a later date, the Kid took Jennie on the floor and the dancing started once more.

Only two men were not dancing, and Joan looked at them. She knew Dusty did not care for dancing, her eyes went to Thackery. Joan had a warm and friendly nature, she had also been a saloongirl for so many years that it was almost second nature to jolly up a miserable looking man. Poor old Claude looked right out of it, for his wife had been almost hauled bodily on to the floor by Borg. Crossing the room, Joan reached out a hand.

"Come on, Claude," she said, in the tones she used so many times under similar circumstances. "Let's show these lead-footed hoppers how it's done."

Although Thackery had always been too busy to learn dancing, Joan was adept at steering such persons around and making them look as if they knew what they were doing. Before the dance had half finished, Thackery was adding fancy little twirls and twists of his own and thoroughly enjoying himself.

At the end of the tune, Thackery ignored his wife's scowls and led Joan to the punchbowl where he began to regale her with tired old jokes. Joan's saloon training had taught her to laugh and appear to be enjoying a customer's efforts to amuse her. So she fed Thackery's ego—and increased Marlene's hatred, which did not worry Joan at all. Marlene was unable to get away from Borg, which probably was just as well.

"Let's have another dance!" Thackery whopped, putting his arm around Joan's waist and hugging her.

"Take it easy, cowboy," Joan grinned, twisting free of his arm. "I'll have no wind left to dance if you hug me like that."

"Now that's an idea," Thackery replied, winking at her. "Then you and I can go out on the porch and sit a spell."

With the skill of a professional saloon pianist, Gaunt saw danger signs in Thackery's actions and his wife's scowls, so began to thump the piano keys.

"Lon," Dusty called, "I'm going up to the room to collect a handkerchief. Do you want me to bring your tobacco? No? I didn't think you would."

"Loncey," Jennie said as Dusty left the room, "I feel a little tired. Will you excuse me. I want to collect my fan from my room."

"Sure, Miss Jennie," the Kid replied.

Dusty had just reached the head of the stairs and was turning on to the passage leading to his room when he heard the patter of feet behind him. At the same moment he heard the sound of a door closing, his room's door or he was no judge of direction. The passage had only a small lamp which gave poor light, for its wick had been turned down.

Nobody should be up on the bedroom floor at this hour of the night and all the people who had any legitimate right to enter the rooms were downstairs. Dusty started forward and thought of the four gunbelts in his room. The prowler had a fair choice of weapons and Dusty was unarmed, except for his bare hands and his feet. Sure, his knowledge of Karate, ju-jitsu and roughhouse brawling gave him an advantage in a fight, but not against a man with a gun.

"Dustine!"

The voice brought him to a halt. He turned and found Jennie coming towards him.

"Should there be anybody up here?" he asked.

"Of course not. The servants all finished work after dinner."

To Dusty it seemed the girl spoke louder than usual. He could see worry lines on her face and wondered what caused them. However, there was the matter of the closing door to be investigated before he took time out to inquire.

"Stay here, Jennie," he ordered and started to cat-foot his way towards the door.

"Dustine!" the girl gasped. "I'm frightened."

The words stopped him in his tracks. Turning, Dusty found the girl approaching with her arms held open. Then she was close to him, arms around his neck and mouth thrust against his, kissing him.

"I'm afraid, Dustine," she gasped into his ear. "I'm afraid of what might happen as a result of Grand-father's will."

Again her mouth found his, kissing him, but he did not kiss back. There had always been something about Jennie which repelled Dusty. He did not know what caused the repulsion, yet he felt it more strongly than ever. Dusty was also puzzled by Jenny's attitude and wondered what caused it. Despite her pallid and fragile appearance, Dusty knew Jennie to have wiry strength and a cold, detached courage. It was most unlike her to be afraid, or to admit to it even if she was.

Gently Dusty eased himself free from the girl's arms and moved her back to arms' length, looking at her face and reading worry if not fear on it.

"Dustine, perhaps one of them might try to kill some of the others to increase their share of Grandfather's money," Jennie gasped as Dusty turned once more towards his room. "They might even kill me!"

"They won't," he replied.

"I—I've seen the way Vint Borg looks at us—and Aunt Marlene and Uncle Claude," she went on. "I'm afraid, Dustine. Please say you'll protect me."

"You know I can't stay here permanently," Dusty answered.

"At least stay for a few days. I'm sure they'll have

made their move before that and you will catch them out. Grandfather always had faith in your ability."

"All right, if it'll make you feel any better I'll stay until Monday. Then I'll have to be heading for home."

Turning, he walked towards his room. The door was closed, just as it had been when he and his *amigos* went downstairs. Standing to one side and against the wall, Dusty reached out, turned the knob and thrust the door open. If anybody was inside Dusty did not intend to give them a nice, clear target at which to shoot.

Nothing happened so Dusty entered, moving cautiously. A lamp on the dressing table shed a faint light, but enough for Dusty to see he had the room to himself. Crossing the room, Dusty turned up the light and looked around him. Everything seemed just as they left it. Walking to the window, Dusty saw it was still fastened on the inside and outside lay a sheer drop. Not even a Rocky Mountain goat could climb the walls of the building.

"What's wrong, Dustine?" Jennie asked from the doorway. "You act like you expected someone in here."

"Where's the key to the cupboard?" he replied. "It was locked when I tried the door."

"The key was lost a long time ago," she answered. "That's why we brought the big wardrobe in here. Whatever you think you saw must have been imagination, Dustine. These passages aren't well-lit and the shadows play tricks."

"You could be right at that," he agreed, collecting a handkerchief from where he had dropped it on the bed.

"Dustine," she said quietly, standing before him. "I—I said a lot of foolish things just now. About—about—you know—I didn't really mean any of them."

"Then why say them?"

"I—I wanted to see you alone, to find out if there is anything between us. If anything could bring us together as Grandfather wished. I can see now it can't come. Please forgive me."

"I do."

"If you wish, you can go home tomorrow."

"Thanks, Jennie. I reckon we'll do that," Dusty drawled. "Come on, let's get downstairs."

On their arrival in the dining room, Dusty and Jennie found another dance in progress, with the Kid standing calling sets. After bringing the dance to a close, the Kid turned and called:

"Hey, Dusty, did you bring my makings?"

"I never thought you'd get round to using them," Dusty replied. "They're the same ones you had when we first met up on the Brownsville trail."*

"I'll go fetch 'em," the Kid grunted. "Getting so a man can't——"

"Who'll dance with me if you go, Lon?" Jennie put in. "You know Dusty doesn't like dancing and everybody else is partnered up."

"If you put it that way, Miss Jennie," grinned the Kid, "I'll just naturally stay on here—happen one of these gents loan me the makings."

For an hour the party went on. Dusty watched Jennie and wondered about her actions. The girl had always been something of a snob, and it surprised Dusty to see her dance with a hired hand, even if the man was one of Ole Devil Hardin's floating outfit. Yet she danced with the Kid and between dances persuaded the other men to loan him tobacco and papers.

Watching the others, Dusty saw that both Borg and Thackery were well on their way to being drunk. Both had punished the punchbowl and the ranch's liquor supply, and neither could take their drink. Borg grew more sneering and insulting. Thackery fawned over Joan in a manner which embarrassed her and the other occupants of the room. More to prevent a scene than for any other reason Mark had started to dance with and entertain Marlene. This did not please Borg, but even as drunk as

---

* Told in *The Ysabel Kid* by J. T. Edson.

he was, the foreman had more sense than tangle with Mark Counter.

Crossing the room, Borg halted at Waco's side as the youngster sat telling a wide-eyed Frankie about some of the things which happened while he helped Dusty run the law in Mulrooney.

"That's it, boy," Borg said, slapping the youngster on the shoulder. "You got it made with that little gal. It ain't everybody can marry young and rich."

While Waco accepted that he would most likely always be the "boy" to Dusty, Mark and the Kid, he objected to any other person calling him by that name. He also did not like having drunks slobber over him.

Coming up from his chair, Waco drove his right fist into Borg's stomach. He had learned fist-fighting from Mark Counter and knew how to throw a punch. The blow caught Borg squarely and folded him over. Up lashed Waco's left fist in a backhand blow which lifted the man erect and set him up for the right cross to the jaw. Borg spun around and crashed to the floor, rolled over once and lay still.

A dull red flush crept to Waco's cheeks as he realized what he had done and that every eye in the room was directed at him.

"Poor old Borg," Mark drawled. "He's done fainted away."

"I figured he'd get around to it," answered the Kid. "Whereat's he sleep, Aunt Mamie?"

"I'll show you," she replied. "Bring him along."

The Kid and Waco took Borg's arms, Mark lifting his legs, and they carried the unconscious foreman from the room, following Mamie to Borg's quarters on the ground floor.

After the men and Mamie left, Marlene had time to see her husband's behavior. Thackery leaned on the side-piece, holding Joan's hand and fixing her, or trying to fix her, with his eyes. To give her her due, Joan tried to get her hand free, but could not.

"Know shomethin', Joanie?" Thackery asked seriously. "My wife doeshn't unnerstan' me."

And telling Joan something she had only heard a couple of thousand times before, Thackery slid to the floor in a limp heap. Joan felt relieved, for the man had been making suggestions which she doubted his wife would approve of should she hear them.

"Reckon we'd best get him to bed, Frank," Dusty drawled. "I reckon the party's over."

"It looks that way," the lawyer admitted. "Take his head, I'll have the feet."

The two men lifted the sleeping Thackery and carried him from the room. Marlene turned and glared at the two girls.

"Get to bed, the pair of you!" she snapped.

Annoyance and anger glinted in Jennie's eyes. In her grandfather's lifetime nobody would have dared speak in such a manner to her inside the walls of Casa Thackery.

"Come on, kids," Joan said quietly, laying a hand on their shoulders. "I'll go up with you."

"You won't!" Marlene snapped. "You and I are going to have a talk in the library."

"We've nothing to say to each other," Joan answered.

"I don't want to say what I have to say in front of the girls, or the other people in this house!" Marlene warned. "But I will if——"

"Have it your own way," Joan sighed. "Go to bed, Frankie."

The four women went into the hall, the girls making for the stairs and Joan walking before Marlene into the library. Jennie, behind her cousin, glanced back at the door and heard the lock click.

"I wonder what they'll do in there," Frankie asked.

"I don't know. Hurry along, Frankie."

"Can I come to your room and talk?"

"Not tonight, dear. I'm very tired. But I'll show you around the house and the range, or some of it, in the morning."

Frankie felt puzzled and a little hurt by her cousin's tone. She had hoped to share a room with Jennie, but the other girl ignored the suggestion when she had made it earlier. It almost seemed as if Jennie did not like her newly arrived younger cousin.

Walking along the passage to her room, Frankie glanced through the door into her Uncle Claude's quarters. Dusty and the lawyer were undressing Thackery and Frankie realized she must not let her Aunt Marlene catch her looking. So Frankie hurried along to her own room and entered. Although she had left the lamp burning low on her dressing table, it appeared to have gone out and the room was dark. However, she had put her night-dress out and could undress in the dark, having done so many times when in Cohen's hands. Then a thought struck her. She could hardly wear her party dress the following morning and so should get the clothes she wore for the journey south.

Hearing voices in the passage, Frankie walked to the door and looked out.

"Dusty," she said. "My lamp's gone out, can you light it for me?"

"Sure," he replied. "It's maybe out of oil though."

On shaking the lamp Dusty heard enough to tell him that shortage of fuel had not been the cause of its going out. Thinking the girl must have turned the wick too low, Dusty took out and lit a match. He raised the glass flame-shield and found the wick high enough to have kept burning. Applying the match's flame to the wick, Dusty twisted the control knob and raised the light volume. He placed the glass cover over the flame and looked around the room.

"Frankie," he said quietly, but urgently. "Go to my

room and bring one of my guns."

"But——"

"Do it, gal!" Dusty snapped, never taking his eyes off the bed.

The girl obeyed. On the trip south she learned to obey without question when Dusty used that tone of voice. Darting across the passage, she entered Dusty's room and took one of the colts from his gunbelt's holsters. The other three Texans were just turning along the passage as she came out and they sprang forward.

"What the hell, Dusty?" Mark asked.

Dusty did not reply. Taking the gun in his right hand, he went towards the bed, gripped the bed-clothes and heaved them back. Throwing the bed-clothes clear, Dusty exposed the coiled shape of a big rattlesnake. Instantly it curled its neck up in an S shape, the evil spade-shaped head drawing back for a strike as its tail buzzed out a warning. Frankie's scream and the crash of Dusty's Colt sounded at the same instant. The headless body of the snake went flying from the bed to land in a coiling, writhing heap on the floor.

"Get the kid out of here!" Dusty snapped to Waco who held the girl, for once without complaint, in his arms. "Take her to her Aunt Mamie."

"Sure, Dusty," Waco replied. "Come on, short-stop, it's all over now."

"How the hell did that get in here?" Mark asked, looking down at the snake. "I've heard of rattlers getting into a bed, but never on the second floor of a stone-built house."

"I don't know," Dusty replied. "Why hasn't the sound of the shot brought the others in here?"

"Don't reckon Thackery'd hear a cannon," grinned the Kid. "And anybody in one of these rooms with the door shut wouldn't hear a thing. Want me to go get the women out of their rooms?"

"No point in disturbing them," Dusty answered.

At that moment the lawyer arrived, running into the room and skidding to a halt, his eyes going to the Colt Dusty held.

"What happened?" he asked. "I saw Waco and Frankie."

"She had a snake in her bed," Mark explained.

"A snake—— But how——?"

"That's what we'd like to know, how it got here," Dusty interrupted. "Sure this is rattler country, but you don't often get them coming into a house like this and getting into a bed."

"It's strange you should say that," Gaunt answered. "One of the Mexican maids was killed by a snake that had climbed into her bed. But that was downstairs on the ground floor."

"When was this?" Dusty asked.

"About a month before Elmo died. The girl's lamp wasn't working, she jumped into bed in the dark and the rattler got her."

At that moment Waco entered the room, throwing a glance at the moving body of the snake.

"Aunt Mamie took care of her," he said. "Got her quietened down a mite. That was a bad shock you gave little short-stop there, Dusty."

"It'd've been a damned sight worse happen she'd climbed into bed, boy," growled the Kid. "Damned if I don't shake my bed out afore I climb in it."

"And me," Mark agreed. "Come on, let's get some sleep. We'll be riding in the morning, won't we, Dusty?"

"I don't know. Maybe we'll stay on for a spell," Dusty replied and turned to Gaunt. "How sound-proof are these rooms, Frank?"

"Near on perfectly. Elmo thought the servants were spying on him and had every room fixed so that you couldn't hear a thing from it once the door was shut. What's wrong, Dusty?"

"Nothing much. We'll have this room cleaned out in

the morning. Now let's get some sleep.''

Although Gaunt noticed nothing, the three cowhands studied Dusty with inquisitive eyes. They knew Dusty very well, too well to be fooled by his casual tones. Dusty was worried, and they wondered what worried him, if his worry was connected with Frankie's narrow escape.

Dusty was worried. Things were taking shape in his head and he did not like the pattern he was beginning to form.

CHAPTER EIGHT

Death In The Night

Joan Shandley sat in the tall-backed chair and watched Marlene Thackery pace the room, halting every few minutes to listen at the door. For almost ten minutes Marlene had walked up and down the library, her long flowing skirt rustling, her bare shoulders white in the light and contrasting with the sleek black of the dress. Each time she turned, the library's hanging lights glinted on the diamond cluster ring she wore.

At last Marlene halted, standing with hands on hips, her magnificent bust rising and falling as she drew in deep breaths.

"You're a cheap looking slut," Marlene finally said. "What did Claude's father see in you?"

"A free meal," Joan answered, determined not be pushed into something she might regret.

"There's no accounting for tastes, I suppose," Marlene went on. "I'd have thought a man as rich as Elmo Thackery could have done better for himself if he had to take a saloon whore."

"You talk like you've had experience," Joan replied.

"Don't think I missed the way you were pawing my husband——"

"I thought it was the other way round; and that you was too busy pawing Vint Borg—or trying to paw Mark Counter."

Marlene's left hand clenched, the light gleaming on

the ring. Only with an effort did she control herself.

"I've an offer to make to you," she gritted out. "It's as much Claude's as mine. My first idea was to have you thrown out of the house, but Claude said we should at least give you enough money to see you on your way. So I'm offering you two thousand dollars to leave this house and never return."

"Two thousand?" Joan replied.

"If you leave tomorrow."

"And if I stay on a few more days I get two hundred and fifty thousand. I don't like your offer, Mrs. Thackery."

"You may as well know my husband is contesting the will," Marlene warned. "With two thousand dollars you could buy a whore-house of your own, until you find some other doddering old fool to sleep with."

"I could buy a better one with two hun——" Joan began, holding the sides of her chair to prevent herself leaping up and attacking the redhead.

"My husband is contesting the will!"

"He has to win his case," Joan pointed out, coming to her feet. "I'll take a chance."

With that Joan started to walk by the other woman, but Marlene shot out a hand, caught her arm and turned her around. Marlene's breasts rose and fell as she drew in short, angry breaths, and hate glowed in her eyes.

"You'll either take my offer!" she hissed, "or I'll make you wish you'd never been born."

"You'll do what?" Joan answered.

"I don't care what you might have been for a couple of nights to the old fool!" Marlene almost screamed. "But no cheap dancehall whore is sharing my money!"

"*Your* money?"

"Mine and my husband's! When I've finished with you——"

"Just hold it, girlie!" Joan cut in savagely. "You can fancy-talk and name-call all you want and get by. But the moment you start face slapping you're playing my game. I've tangled with girls tough enough to make you look like a plate full of mush."

"Have you?" purred Marlene.

For a moment Joan thought Marlene would back down and call off the fight before it came to physical violence. Then without any warning Marlene swung her right hand around in a slap that sent Joan sprawling on to the settee.

"That's just for a start, whore," Marlene said. "Now I'm going to teach you respect for your betters."

Jumping forward, she dragged up her skirt to above her shapely knees and drew back her right leg. It lashed forward, straight into Joan's hands as the little woman thrust herself up from the settee. Gripping Marlene's ankle, Joan gave it a jerking twist. Marlene lost her balance and fell over, landing on and breaking her fall with her hands, the leg still trapped. With a heave, Joan stood the other woman on her head, allowing her skirt and petticoats to fall around her waist, exposing her black stocking clad legs and frilly garters to view. Shoving the trapped leg from her, Joan let the woman fall on to her back. Joan moved around to stand before Marlene and put a hand up to touch the mark left by Marlene's fingers on her cheek.

"Give it up while you're ahead," she warned. "From now I'm fighting back."

Marlene sat on the floor and spat out a mouthful of curses, all her veneer of refinement falling away. On getting to her feet she stood facing Joan who crouched lightly on the balls of her feet, fists clenched ready to defend herself. For a moment they faced each other, then Marlene started to turn away from Joan. A faint smile came to Joan's lips as she also started to turn. It looked like Mrs. Thackery did not aim to take the matter further.

Bunching her left hand into a fist, Marlene whirled around and lashed a blow at Joan's head. The smaller woman caught the start of the move and made a bad mistake. She turned around, straight into Marlene's fist. Smashing into Joan's cheek, the cluster of diamonds gashed the flesh and the force of the blow spun Joan around, dropping her face down on the floor. Joan lay there, dizzy and partly stunned by the blow, helpless for the moment.

Luckily for Joan, Marlene knew little about the rudiments or refinements of hair-yanking brawls. Instead of smashing both knees down on the defenseless woman's back, Marlene hauled her skirts up and dropped to kneel astride Joan. Digging her hands into Joan's hair, Marlene began to pull, at the same time forcing Joan's face down into the carpet.

Pain cleared Joan's head and she knew she must do something before she lost her hair and scalp-skin too. Bracing herself, Joan forced her body up on hands and knees. Marlene gasped, releasing Joan's hair with her left hand to swing it at the other woman's head and back. The ring hurt when it landed and Joan knew she must get rid of it or sustain serious injury.

Using all her strength, Joan rolled Marlene over so the redhead landed on her side. Pure instinct caused Marlene to close her legs, locking them around Joan's middle. Her left hand reached around Joan's head to try to claw at her face while the right one gripped the neck of Joan's dress and tore at it, ripping open the fastenings. Joan grabbed the left wrist, trying to get the ring off, but Marlene clenched her hand into a fist. Not to be beaten, Joan dragged the hand to her mouth and bit at the base of the thumb. Marlene screamed, her fingers opened and her other hand beat a tattoo at Joan's head. Twisting the ring from Marlene's finger, Joan threw it across the room to land in the hearth by the fire. Marlene's legs opened and Joan rolled free.

Twisting around and on to her knees, Joan flung herself at Marlene as the bigger woman lay holding her bleeding hand and screaming. Joan landed on Marlene, one hand digging into and ruining the neatly coiffured

red hair, the other driving into Marlene's face and body.
Pain came to Marlene's rescue this time. With a heave
of her body, she rolled Joan over and landed on top.

For almost ten minutes the two women rolled and
thrashed over and over on the floor. Despite her extra
size and weight, Marlene got the worst of the fight, for
she had never before engaged in physical combat while
Joan had experience gained in a dozen barroom brawls
to back her and make up for her lack of size.

They came to their knees, gasping, squealing and
lunging at each other. More by accident than design,
Marlene's hands closed on Joan's throat and clung to it.
Then the big woman forced herself to her feet, still
holding Joan by the neck and ignoring the hard little
fists which thudded into her body.

Joan was desperate, for the grip on her throat cut
off her air and she could not breathe. Then Marlene
released her, giving up a hold which would have ended
the fight so as to grab Joan's hair and use it as a means
to throw the smaller woman across the room. Joan
landed on the settee and rolled off it as Marlene hurled
herself forward. The big woman landed where Joan had
been and was dragged to the floor by the legs to resume
the fight.

Never had Joan been in such a brutal, savage fight.
Marlene fought with the strength of hatred, if she had
been skilled too it would have gone hard for Joan. Even
without skill, Marlene's strength gave her an advantage
and she handed brutal punishment to the other woman
although Joan gave back as good as she got.

At last, almost half an hour after the first blow
landed, Joan rolled a weakly struggling Marlene flat on
to her back and knelt astride her. They had fought with
fists, feet, elbows, knees and teeth, tearing hair, punch-
ing, slapping, clawing, pushing each other across the
room. Both were naked to the waist, the upper parts of
their frocks either hanging around their hips, or lying on
the floor; their skirts torn; shoes gone and stockings

in tatters; blood flowed from noses, lips, bites and scratches, and each body had a mottling of bruises.

Gripping Marlene's hair in her hands, Joan lifted the red head and banged it on the floor. Marlene struggled weakly, her hands coming up to dig claws into Joan's shoulders. Again Joan raised Marlene's head and drove it down. Four times in all she crashed Marlene's head to the floor, the hands fell away from her and the struggles ended.

"I—I—told—you——!" Joan gasped, trying to rise.

She could not. Waves of pain and exhaustion welled through her, all she could do was rest her hands on the floor and try to support her aching body. A distant squeaking rumble came to Joan's ears, but she had not the energy to turn her head and see what caused the noise.

Suddenly a brilliant flash of light seemed to explode before Joan's eyes, then everything sank off into blackness and she collapsed to the floor.

"You're getting old, Joan," a voice seemed to be saying, "letting a fat bladder like her whip you."

Then dull aching pain filled her body and she tried to lift her head from the carpet on which she lay. Joan had been knocked unconscious before and knew the symptoms. She waited for her head to stop spinning and tried to think straight. Memory came back to her, she remembered sitting astride Marlene and wondered where the redhead gained that last reserve of strength to throw her off and deliver a finishing blow.

A shock of fear hit Joan, the room was dark— perhaps Marlene had—no, it was only that the room's lamps had died down through lack of fuel and that her left eye had swollen shut.

One of Joan's hands struck against something as it fumbled on the floor. Without looking, she raised the hand and felt at the thing, recognizing the touch of human flesh. Lifting her head with an effort, she looked along her arms which extended before her. Something glinted on one hand, but she felt too exhausted to look what it might be. It took all Joan's will-power to keep her head up and examine the thing her hand rested on. Her eyes took in a shapely leg with a tattered stocking hanging below its knee and a garter making a slash of color against the white flesh of the thigh. A second leg bent up in the air beyond the first, one which was bare and had a dull, rusty red streak running down its calf.

"She must have collapsed as soon as she finished me off," Joan thought with relief "That explains why she didn't scratch my eyes out."

Slowly Joan's eyes went along the legs to where they emerged from the torn black skirt. Passing the skirt, she looked along Marlene's dirty, bruised torso, over the rich full breasts towards the throat, then jerked back towards the breasts again. Something rose from under the left breast—it took Joan only a moment to recognize that something for what it was.

"Oh, my god!" she gasped.

Weakly she forced herself to her feet, never taking her eyes from the knife hilt which rose under Marlene's left breast. Turning, Joan stumbled blindly across the room and to the door. After tugging at the knob for a few seconds, Joan remembered Marlene had locked them in on entering. Her fingers did not seem able to obey the dictates of her mind, but she managed to turn the key at last and open the door.

The hall outside lay dark and still. Joan did not know which way to go or what to do. At first she thought of flight, leaving the house and fleeing before she could be blamed for the killing. Common sense came to her aid, she would not make half a mile in her present condition; half naked, bare footed and battered so badly.

Turning, she made her way to the stairs and dragged herself up them. Only one man could save her, prove that she had not killed Marlene. Joan could barely stand, her lungs seemed ready to burst as she staggered to and opened the door of the Texans' room.

Always a light sleeper, the Kid woke as the door opened, reaching a hand to the lamp by the bed and turning up its wick to flood the room with light.

"What the hell!" he growled.

The other three were awake by that time and every eye went to the shape at the door. There was no time to think of personal modesty, or the proprieties of allowing a woman to see them undressed. All four men swung from their beds, grabbing and donning their pants with speed.

"It—it's the Thack—Thackery dame——" Joan gasped, stumbling forward. "We h-had a fight."

"Looks that way," replied the Kid, springing forward to catch her as she collapsed and easing her down on to his bed.

"Go wake Aunt Mamie, Waco!" Dusty ordered. "We'd best get downstairs and see how bad hurt Marlene is."

"If she's roughed as bad as Joan, she's in poor shape," Mark replied, pouring water from the jug on the washstand into its bowl. "It must have been one hell of a fight."

"Marlene's been spoiling for it since they first met," the Kid answered.

"Sure," agreed Mark. "You pair get downstairs. I'll tend to Joan."

Knowing Mark had a considerable knowledge of treating fistfight injuries, Dusty gave his agreement and left the room followed by the Kid. They met Waco and Mamie at the stairhead, the old woman carrying a lamp.

"We didn't wake Frankie," she said. "What's wrong?"

Mamie Thackery had lived all her life in the West and ignored the state of dress shown by all three men, for she guessed something serious was afoot. She wore a robe over her nightdress and had a sleeping cap on her head, but none of the men even glanced at it.

"There's been some trouble," Dusty replied and led

the way downstairs to the library door.

Entering the room first, Dusty saw enough to tell him there had been bad trouble. Not only were the chairs turned over, the carpets rucked up and the table disarranged, swung at an angle to where it usually stood, but he could see Marlene's body sprawled on the floor. Dusty saw more than just the body. Enough to make him thrust out an arm and stop the old woman entering the room.

"Stay out there for a moment, Aunt Mamie," he ordered.

"What is it Dusty?" she replied, but obeyed him.

"Trouble. Lon, go get dressed, and you, boy."

Crossing the room, Dusty bent by the woman's body. He had no eye for her shapely breasts as such for he knew they belonged to a corpse. Dropping a hand, Dusty touched the cold flesh, then he rose and walked across the room, through the door, closing it behind him.

"Lon!" he called. "Saddle up and head for Thackery City. Get the sheriff out here as fast as you can."

Not for the first time Dusty felt grateful for having friends who would obey orders without asking any questions. The Kid gave a wave and carried on up the stairs out of sight, Waco on his heels.

"What's happened, Dustine?" Mamie asked.

"There's been a fight. Not just a yelling fight, but cat-clawing. Marlene's dead," Dusty answered, then put out his hand to catch and steady the old woman. "Easy there, Aunt Mamie. There's nothing we can do and I want that room leaving just as it is until the law comes. Where's the key?"

Gently he eased Mamie down into a chair and for a moment she made no reply to his question. With an effort Dusty could almost see the old woman take a hold of herself and looked up at him.

"Marlene asked me for it shortly before the party broke up. She said she wanted to sleep downstairs to teach Claude a lesson and didn't want him coming to her until morning.''

Turning, Dusty opened the door, he found the key in the lock, removed it and closed the door to lock it from the outside. Then he turned to the old woman and laid a hand gently on her shoulder.

"Did—did Joan kill her?" Mamie asked.

"It looks that way," Dusty replied.

"Why? For the money?"

"They'd been fighting, a hell of a fight, not just a slap, hair-yank and run away crying brawl. Maybe Joan struck out in self-defense, she was a lot lighter than Marlene."

"I liked Joan. She was so friendly——"

"Sure," Dusty answered. "Do you reckon we'd best wake Claude?"

"I don't think we could, not with the amount he drank during the evening."

Before either could say more, the Kid and Waco came clattering down the stairs, both fully dressed and armed, Waco carrying Dusty's shirt, socks and boots.

"Tell Lon how to find Thackery City, Aunt Mamie," Dusty ordered, taking the shirt and drawing it on.

"Just follow the trail to the east, Lon," she explained. "Sheriff Topham lives in a white frame house on the edge of town as you go in."

"Yo!" replied the Kid and left the house.

"Mark sent this down, Dusty," Waco said and dropped a ring into the small Texan's palm.

"It's the one Marlene bought in Mulrooney," Dusty snapped. "Where did you get it, boy?"

"Mark took it from Joan's finger just now."

CHAPTER NINE

Death in a Locked Room—Twice

"It looks like an open and shut case to me," Sheriff Brendan Topham announced judicially as he followed Dusty Fog from the library to face Mamie and Dusty's three *amigos*.

The time was half past four in the morning and Topham had just completed examining Marlene Thackery's body and the library. Topham was a tall, thin, miserable looking man, poorly dressed and not too bright. However, he came cheap and this had been the main reason for the county commissioners hiring him; Elmo Thackery ran the county commissioners with his usual tight-fisted regard for money.

"Does, huh?" grunted the Ysabel Kid.

Always a great one for first impressions, the Kid did not possess a high regard for the sheriff on their first meeting and nothing seen so far caused him to revise his opinion.

"Sure, that dancehall gal knifed Mrs. Thackery——"

"Who said Joan was a dancehall girl?" Dusty put in.

"I heard Elmo tell about her when he come back from that trail drive. Reckon I'll go upstairs and haul her off to jail."

"Just like that?" Mark growled.

"How'd you mean, young feller?" Topham answered. "She killed Mrs. Th——"

143

"And you stood by and let her?"

Eyeing Mark for a long moment while he thought over the meaning of the big Texan's words, Topham finally gave it up.

"How'd mean? I wasn't there to stop it."

"Then how'd you know Joan did it?" Mark asked. "I always heard that folks were considered innocent until proven guilty."

"What's wrong down there?" asked Jennie from the head of the stairs.

"Nothing you can help with," Dusty replied. "Go back to bed."

Ignoring Dusty's words, the girl came downstairs and looked at the library door. Then she turned her pallid face to Dusty.

"There's something happened. In that room. I knew there would be trouble when they locked the door after them."

"Who?" Dusty asked.

"Aunt Marlene and Miss Shandley. They went into the library after the party ended. Aunt Marlene sent Francine and I to bed. I heard the lock click as I went upstairs. What's happened, Dustine?"

A triumphant leer came to Topham's face as he heard Jennie's words and read the meaning behind them. One of the first things he did when entering the library was to check that all the windows remained fastened on the inside.

"It looks like we got an open and shut case again," he said.

"Dustine!" Jennie's voice raised a trifle. "What *has* happened?"

"You'd best tell her, Aunt Mamie," Dusty answered, then turned to Topham. "Let's go hear what Joan has to say before you toss her in jail."

Although he would have preferred to question Joan privately, Topham found the four Texans on his heels as he entered her room, where Mark had carried her after cleaning her wounds. Joan woke as the Kid lit the lamp, and stared around her. Seeing the sheriff's badge, cold fear hit her and she wanted to scream her innocence even though he, from his appearance, would not believe her.

"I'm taking you in for murder," Topham announced with relish.

There had never been a murder while he held office and this one looked like it ought to attract attention even in the East. Topham had heard that Eastern newspapermen sometimes bought stories from Western lawmen and he could always use money, for the county did not pay him very well.

"She's not being moved," Mark put in quietly.

"Now look here, young feller——" Topham began.

"Suppose we hear Joan's story first," Dusty interrupted. "Knowed a sheriff once, he had him what looked like a certain suspect to a crime. Was so sure about it he arrested the man and sent him for trial. Only trouble then was that the man proved his innocence and sued the county for false arrest. He won his case and the county got itself a new sheriff."

Apparently Topham had enough sense to work out the moral of Dusty's story. While he might understand it, Topham did not like it. Scowling at the four Texans, he hoped to send them from the room while the girl said her piece.

Speaking slowly and weakly, Joan told the sheriff and cowhands—who had not taken Topham's hint—of the fight and what led up to it. She felt scared, for she knew no small town jury would believe her story and would find her guilty. A saloongirl would have no chance at all in a place like Thackery City.

"You say you thought you'd knocked her cold?" Dusty asked at the end of Joan's story. "You were kneeling astride her, banging her head on the floor.

Then she hit you over the head and when you recovered she had the knife in her.''

"It's the truth, Dusty!" Joan gasped. "May I never move from here if it's not. I didn't kill her."

"Open and shut case," grunted Topham. "That door was locked on the inside. Only the two of 'em in the room. She had to be the one who done it."

"Did she?"

Once more Topham looked hard at Mark as the blond giant asked a question.

"Who else could have?"

"You've a real good point there, sheriff," drawled Mark. "Only Joan couldn't have done it. You take a look on the top of her head. There's a helluva lump on it. Happen she caught a crack hard enough to raise that she wouldn't be doing anything for a fair time."

"Mrs. Thackery hit her!" Topham answered.

"You saw that wound," Dusty put in. "Straight to the heart. Are you telling me that Marlene Thackery picked up that chair leg that was beside her, hit Joan with it, after she was knifed?"

"How many men have you killed with a knife, sheriff?" asked the Kid.

"What—how many—none!"

"I have, a few, and I'll tell you one thing for sure. Whoever used that knife'd get splashed with blood. On the hand holding the knife for certain, maybe on the chest. Blood'd spurt out of the wound, even with the knife in it."

"And there was no blood on Joan's hands or body, not enough for that," Mark went on. "But you'll have to take my word for that. I cleaned her up."

"Why'd you do that?" snapped Topham suspiciously.

"Because I didn't know there'd been a killing when I started to clean her. By the time I heard it was too late. Just take a look at the lump on Joan's head."

Grudgingly, Topham bent forward and Joan lowered her head. Even through the tangled hair, the lump showed plainly. From its appearance, Joan had taken a hard enough knock to render her unconscious for some time. Yet Topham still sought for excuses, not wanting to let a promising case slip through his fingers, nor have it become so complicated that he would never solve it.

"Maybe she fell d——" he began.

"How'd she do that?" Waco asked. "Stand on the table and dive head first?"

"Or put her head down and charge at the wall like a big-horn ram fighting for a lil gal sheep?" drawled the Kid mildly, which in his case sounded more sarcastic than if he had sneered the words out.

From the position on her head, Joan would have been unable to deliver such a blow as needed to raise that bump. Topham saw this, after it had been pointed out forcibly to him.

"She has to be the one——" he groaned.

"Happen you feel that way," Dusty said. "I'll go wake Frank Gaunt and ask him to act for Miss Shandley."

The mention of Gaunt's name brought a sudden change in Topham's attitude. All too well the sheriff knew Gaunt's legal reputation, and he had no wish to endanger his case against Joan by making trouble for her lawyer.

"Naw, I'll leave it lie until morning," he started. "Don't go disturbing Mr. Gaunt's sleep."

"Then let's get out of here and let Miss Joan get some sleep," Dusty suggested. "She won't try to escape."

It never occurred to Mark, the Kid and Waco to disobey any order—for order and not suggestion it had been—Dusty gave. They left the room and the sheriff went along with them.

"Whyn't you mention the ring, Dusty?" Mark asked as they followed the other men to the stairhead.

"Then he'd be sure Joan killed Marlene."

"He's sure now."

"Yep. But that'd give him a stronger motive. We know Joan, Mark. She might get into a fight with Marlene, if Marlene pushed her and I reckon she did. But she wouldn't kill and she wouldn't steal the ring. Even if she stole it, Joan'd be a damned sight too smart to wear it."

"You're the boss," Mark drawled. "I'll go along with you about Joan not stealing it. Only how the hell did all this happen? I mean, if Joan didn't kill Marlene, who did?"

"I don't know."

On their way down to the ground floor, the men met Mamie and Jennie who were on their way to bed. Dusty stopped the women, seeing that Jennie did not appear to be unduly worried by her aunt's death.

"Will you come down with us, Aunt Mamie?" he asked. "We'd like to look around the room. I've had M—the body covered with a sheet."

"I'll come," Mamie replied.

"So will I," Jennie went on. "Don't worry, Dustine. I can face it. I know I may seem callous, but I didn't know Aunt Marlene very well and doubt if we would ever have become friends."

"Sure," Dusty answered, watching the girl's face. "You know the house better than anybody other than Aunt Mamie, so you may be able to help us."

In the room, Dusty set his pards searching, checking that the windows' fastenings did their work properly. He asked Jennie if she was sure about hearing the lock click and she stated firmly that she had heard it.

"Nothing, Dusty," Mark said at last. "Every window's held firm from inside."

"Say," the Kid put in. "This here's an old Spanish place, isn't it?"

"Built by the *Conquistodores*," Jennie replied, a note of pride in her voice.

"Remember Casa Almonte, Dusty?" asked the Kid.

"Sure——You mean that secret passage behind the walls?"

"Yep, that's just what I mean."

"How about it, Aunt Mamie?" Dusty asked. "Do you know of any secret passages in the house?"

"I've never seen or heard of any, Dusty. Of course, Elmo had been living here for almost a year before he brought me in as housekeeper. Do you know of any, Jennie?"

If anybody in the house knew about secret passages Jennie would be that person. Although he treated his sister Mamie little better than a hired housekeeper and told her nothing of his business, Thackery had doted on Jennie and never held anything back from her.

"No, Aunt Mamie," the girl replied, her face impassive and uninterested. "There are none."

"Are you sure, Jennie?" Dusty asked.

"Of course I am!" Jennie snapped. "If there had been, Grandfather would have told me about them."

"It looks bad for the sal——" Topham began.

"Mister, that gal up there is one of the legatees for the Thackery will," Dusty cut in. "Let's save this until morning."

Topham watched Dusty's face, wondering if the small Texan was joking about Joan having a share in the Thackery fortune. Nothing about Dusty said he exercised his cowhand sense of humour and so Topham concluded Dusty spoke the truth.

"Undertaker'll be here in the morning, and the doctor," he grunted, not saying what he thought. "I'd be obliged if you'd stay on for the inquest and trial Cap'n Fog."

"We'll do that," Dusty replied. "Now let's get some sleep. Lock the door of the library and keep the key, sheriff. Let's go."

Breakfast at Casa Thackery proved to be a sober meal, far different from dinner the previous night. At the head of the table a black-dressed Claude Thackery moodily stirred a cup of coffee. He had been told of his wife's death and while he looked shocked, he did not seem to be over-grieving. Mark, the Kid and Waco, the two girls, Gaunt and Topham shared the table. All looked towards the door as Dusty and Mamie entered. The old woman's face showed the strain she was under, but she seemed to be steady enough.

"I told Joan to stay in her room," Dusty said as he came to the table.

"We thought it would be best," Mamie went on. "Where's Vint?"

"He's not awake yet, Aunt Mamie," Jennie replied. "I sent one of the maids to call him."

At that moment, the room door flew open and a terrified-looking Mexican girl burst in, ran to the table and began to babble in such rapid Spanish that only the Ysabel Kid could follow her words. The others could catch a word here and there, but not enough to make sense of what she said.

"What is it, Lon?" Dusty asked as the lean, Indian-dark youngster came to his feet.

"The gal allows Borg's lying on the floor in his room—with a gun in his hand and a pool of blood around his head."

"Go check, Mark, Waco," Dusty snapped, then realized that the county sheriff should be giving the orders.

"Hold hard!" Topham yelped, rising from his chair and looking around in a bewildered manner. "I'll come with you."

His words went to the departing backs of the two cowhands, for they had not waited around on hearing Dusty's orders.

Turning, Dusty looked to where Mamie and the Kid had succeeded in quietening the girl. She sat rigid in a chair, shivering with fear, teeth chattering, but could speak clearly when Dusty asked her how she came to see Borg.

"Did you go into his room?" he asked.

"N-no, *senor*," the girl replied. "I knock. I try the door. It is locked. Often before it has been locked and I go to the side window, where I make noise and wake Senor Vint. This morning his window she is fasten. I look in and see him. He lies on the floor with a—with a——"

"All right, Rosita," Mamie said quietly, taking the girl into her arms.

Dusty threw a look at the two girls. Francine sat with eyes wide open and fear on her face, but Jennie showed no emotion, which was about what he expected.

"Look after the women, Frank," he said to the lawyer. "I'll go see what's happening. Come on, Lon."

Followed by the Kid, Dusty left the room. Thackery still sat at the head of the table and he thought what Borg's death meant. Taken with Marlene's demise, it meant over five hundred thousand extra dollars to be divided between the survivors. Then another thought struck him. Suppose one of the others intended to be the last survivor and take the lot? At that moment Claude Thackery started to think of getting out of Casa Thackery as soon as he could, or surrounding himself with bodyguards who would ensure his safety.

Borg's quarters lay at the end of a passage on the ground floor. The room was as large as the one allocated to the Texans and furnished in much the same manner.

On arrival Dusty found the door had been burst in. He entered the room and saw Waco examining the window's fastenings while Mark and Topham bent over the ranch foreman's body. It lay sprawled out on the floor, face down and feet pointing towards the bed, a Colt Cavalry Peacemaker gripped ready for shooting in the right hand. On carrying Borg to bed the previous night, Mark and the others had not troubled to undress him, but laid him on his bed fully clothed, the body still had its clothes on. There was a small hole, blackened and burned by exploding gunpowder, in the center of the back of the head. Dusty did not need to look at the front, he could imagine the hideous mess the bullet would have made when it shattered its way out.

"The windows are fastened on the inside," Waco announced. "And the key's in the lock at this side, been turned."

"We didn't lock the door," Mark stated. "But I remember seeing the key in the lock."

"What do you make of it, sheriff?" Dusty asked.

"Suicide, what else?"

Stepping forward, Dusty looked down at the body. A frown creased Dusty's brow as he studied the gun. Then he turned to the sheriff and took out his left hand Colt, offering it to Topham but first.

"Show me how he did it."

"Huh?" croaked the alarmed sheriff.

"I don't mean cock the hammer and shoot, just hold the gun and point it at the back of your head so that if you shot the bullet'd go through at the same angle as Borg's."

Determined to show that soft-spoken short cowhand once and for all who was sheriff in these danged parts, Topham took the gun and raised it towards his head. He held the gun normally, forefinger on the trigger, other three fingers and thumb curled around the butt. A snag became immediately obvious as he lifted the gun. No matter how he tried, Topham could not place the barrel of the Colt against his head in such a manner that it would send the bullet through at the same angle as the one which killed Borg took.

"And that's only a Civilian Model you're holding," Dusty remarked as the baffled looking sheriff lowered the gun. "Borg's gun has the Cavalry Model barrel."

Handing back Dusty's gun, Topham frowned in a pain-filled manner which indicated he was thinking. He looked around the room in a bewildered manner and shook his head as if the entire business was beyond him.

"He couldn't have shot his-self," was Topham's brilliant deduction. "But who could have?"

"That's something we'll have to find out," Dusty answered.

Crossing the room, Dusty opened its cupboard door. Like the cupboard in his room, this one also had been built into the wall. Dusty examined the stone bricks, trying to find signs of a door leading into a secret passage. He saw nothing to tell that other than a solid wall backed the cupboard and the floor looked equally firm. Borg's clothes hung on pegs, boots and other gear lay on the floor, and his gunbelt, its holster empty, hung on a hook behind the door.

"Nothing," he said. "Let's go back to the dining room."

The three cowhands followed Dusty from the room, Topham threw a final look around and followed them into the passage.

"Wished I'd got me a deputy here to guard this room," he hinted.

His hint was not taken, the four cowhands carried on walking. With a sigh, Topham went back into the room to wait until the undertaker and doctor arrived from town.

Gaunt had the room to himself when the four Texans returned. Sitting at his table, his head resting on his hands, the lawyer looked bewildered and shocked by the events of the past few hours.

"I asked Mamie to take the maid to her room, Frankie went with her," the lawyer said, lifting his head. "Claude's gone to his room. I get the feeling he's not as unhappy about his wife's death as he might be."

"Where's Jennie?" Dusty asked.

"I don't know. Maybe went to help her aunt. You never know with that girl, she flits about the house like a ghost," the lawyer replied. "What happened?"

"Borg was murdered," Dusty replied quietly.

"Murdered!" Gaunt gasped.

"Yep. Made to look like suicide. Might have worked if only Topham'd been looking into it."

"Huh, huh!" grunted the lawyer, having a low, if accurate, opinion of Topham as a sheriff. "But who——"

"We don't know," Dusty replied. "Or how. Frank, where's Elmo Thackery's grave?"

"He's not been buried."

"Why not?"

"The ravine he fell into is right out of the way on the back range country. It'd've been risky, too risky, to try to get the body out; one slip and the man going down would have been impaled on needle-sharp rocks. There was a clause in the will which read, as near as I can remember, 'I ask that if my death occurs on a place where my body will not endanger human health, or offend living people's eyes, let it lie without burial, for I do not wish to be buried underground.' The ravine's well clear of human beings, so we accepted his last wish and left him there. Had the local preacher out and he read the burial ceremony, then we left the body where it fell."

More and more the parts of the puzzle fell into place. Dusty could see almost everything. A visit to the ravine where Thackery met his end would either clear up the situation, or blow it up into the air.

"Go get the cook to bring some food in, boy," Dusty ordered. "After we've ate, Mark, you, Lon and I're taking a ride."

"How about me?" Waco asked.

"You stay here and guard the women."

"Do you think the killer might try again, in daylight, Dusty?" Gaunt inquired, watching the young Texan and wondering if he had ever seen Dusty so grim and serious before.

"I don't know. All I know is I don't aim to take any chances."

After Waco left for the kitchen, Mark asked, "Where're we riding?"

"Out to where Elmo died. I figure we ought to show our respects. How do we find the place, Frank?"

With a meal under their belts, Dusty, Mark and the Kid took their horses and rode from Casa Thackery. Waco watched them go, wondering why Dusty borrowed a piece of his working equipment. Wishing he was riding with his *amigos*, Waco tended to his big paint stallion. He noticed a fast little grulla gelding which had been in one of the stalls was no longer there, but thought little about it. Possibly one of the hands took it out to graze.

Waco spent almost an hour with the horse, then headed to the house to find Gaunt in the company of the sheriff, doctor and undertaker. Turning to the young Texan, Gaunt said:

"Can you collect the ladies and bring them to the dining room, Waco?"

"Sure," he replied. "Are they in their rooms?"

"Mamie and Frankie are with Miss Shandley," answered Gaunt.

On delivering his message to the women, Waco found that Mamie had a will of her own.

"Joan's not leaving this bed. You tell Brendan Topham to come up here and ask any questions he has for us. Frankie, go and tell your cousin Jennie I want to see her here."

"Yes'm," Frankie answered, looking worried.

"I'll take you, short-stop," Waco smiled, ruffling her hair.

At any other time his action and the name would have brought a wave of protest from the girl. But Frankie was so shaken by the events of the past hours that she did not feel like trying to flirt or have fun.

Her feelings did not improve when she and Waco arrived at Jennie's door and, after knocking several times, tried the door to find it locked.

"D-do you think——!" Frankie gasped.

"I don't think anything," Waco replied. "But I'd sure like to look inside."

Fumbling in her hair, Frankie extracted a bobby-pin and bent over the lock. Waco tried to see what she was doing, but could not. When Frankie straightened up, she turned the knob and the door opened.

"Where in hell did you learn a trick like that?" Waco growled.

"Cohen taught us how to do it, for when we worked as maids in hotels."

"Let me go in first," he ordered.

To tell the truth Waco did not relish what might be waiting for him in the room. However, he pushed open the door and entered. The room, without a doubt the best and most luxuriously furnished in the house, was empty.

"She's not here," Waco said and the little girl entered.

"Th-that's the hem of her dress under the bed!" she gasped.

"Easy there, short-stop. That's the one she wore last night. She had another on this morning."

Crossing the room, Waco bent and pulled the dress from under the bed. On seeing it to be only a dress, Frankie came forward to take it from his hands. It might make Jennie like her more if she folded the dress, so she started to do so.

"What's this on the front?" she asked, her fingers feeling something which turned the cloth stiff and gritty to the touch.

"Let me look," Waco replied, retrieving the dress and examining the spot.

"Let's go, Frankie," he said after his inspection.

"What is it, Waco?" she gasped.

"Nothing. Jennie spilled something on her dress, that's all."

But that was not all. Even though he sounded truthful and kept his voice even, Waco had lied to the girl. The stiff patch on the front of Jennie's dress had been caused by a lot of blood congealing.

CHAPTER TEN

Captain Fog Pays His Respects to
Elmo Thackery

Following Gaunt's instructions, Dusty, Mark and the Kid had little difficulty in finding their way across the range and to the bush-covered slope up which Elmo Thackery rode to his doom. There had been considerable coming and going in the area and the point where Thackery's body went over was much flattened down by many feet.

Leaving the three stallions standing free, for none would stray far, Dusty and the other two walked cautiously to the edge of the ravine and looked down at the shape on the rocks. One glance told them why nobody had attempted to bring up the body for burial. The walls fell sheer and down below the jagged rocks spread over the bottom so that a single slip would mean death for the man who went down to try and bring out the body. Nothing about the body had changed, no animals could get down into the ravine to worry at it and the turkey buzzards appeared to have missed locating the feed which lay in the dark and gloomy bottom of the ravine.

"Looks like him," drawled the Kid. "Way I remember him."

"Sure," Dusty replied. "Collect those ropes and let's make a start."

In addition to their own ropes, Dusty had borrowed Waco's before leaving the ranch. Each rope was forty foot long, made of three strand, hard-plaited Manila fiber, and strong enough to halt the rush of a fleeing longhorn steer. Although the ravine was not more than a hundred foot deep, Dusty brought Waco's rope to ensure they had sufficient for their purpose.

"Let me go down instead of you, Dusty," suggested the Kid. "And I'm only asking because I know you'll say no."

"I'm lighter than you," Dusty replied. "Every ounce'll count when I get to the bottom, there'll be the weight of rope above me adding to the strain then."

"Allus wanted to die young," grinned the Kid. "You make sure of them knots, Mark. Dusty's got my makings in his pocket."

"You never take them out and offer them round anyway," Mark answered, fastening two of the ropes together.

For all his light-hearted reply, Mark made sure the ropes were securely knotted and would not pull apart at their joining place. A sailor could teach a cowhand little or nothing about tying knots, and Mark was exceptionally skilled at the art.

"All done," he said, after setting his foot on one rope and tugging on the other to test its knot. Crossing to the edge of the ravine, he looked down then raised his eyes to Dusty's face. "Whooee! That's a mean looking spot for a man to drop into."

"If you get any more happy thoughts like that," Dusty replied, "do us both a favor and keep them to yourself."

With that Dusty picked the end of the first rope and slid the honda down to form a loop into which he placed his right foot. Dusty tested the honda—a spliced, leather-wrapped eyelet at the end of the rope and used for making the loop—to ensure it would hold firm. Satisfied it would, he stood at the edge of the ravine, placed his foot into the loop and drew tight, took the rope up between his crotch, twisted it around his body and gripped firmly with his hands.

"All set?" asked Mark.

"Ten or fifteen years ago'd be better," Dusty answered.

Sitting on the rough edge of the ravine, Dusty looked to Mark, nodded, and eased himself off. Mark braced his feet apart and took the strain, paying the rope out slowly and evenly. Below Dusty lay a hundred foot drop and sharp rocks just waiting to claim another victim. He could see skeletons of cattle, antelope and other animals which had blundered into the death trap. No wonder the coroner's inquest found Thackery's death tragic but not unexpected. The old man's horse had been frightened by something, reared and threw him from the saddle to fall to his death. If Mark made a slip, the ravine would claim another human victim.

Standing close to the edge of the ravine, Mark allowed the rope to slide through his fingers slowly, letting Dusty sink down into the murky depths below. The strain would get worse, for he could not let the rope slide down over the edge of the ravine. It was so jagged that the fibers might be cut or weakened so as to break and send Dusty plunging to his death. That was why the lowering could not be done by their horses, only Mark's giant strength could handle the chore in safety.

While Mark worked, the Ysabel Kid kept a watch on the ropes, ready to warn when a knot came, for it would take careful handling to slip one past Mark's grip without losing his hold on the even running rope. Pure instinct caused the Kid to draw and hold his rifle, and his senses stayed alert all the time. A man did not spend his formative years as the Kid had without developing the caution of a much-hunted lobo wolf.

"Watch that knot, Mark!" he said.

"Got it," Mark replied a moment after.

The three big stallions stood to one side. Blackie, the Kid's white stallion, was a short way from the other two. Like its master, the white had many wild traits and its alertness had been put to good use by the Kid in the days when he ran contraband with his father along the Rio Grande. Always the big stallion stayed watchful, ready to give warning of the scent, sight or sound of approaching human beings.

Such a scent came to the horse's nostrils, faintly, but drawing closer and taking a pattern Blackie recognized. Fear has its own smell, so has a hunting creature's body odor. A hunting human being crept nearer and nearer, its scent carried by the wind to the white's nostrils.

Throwing back its head, the white snorted, looking to where the scent originated. The Kid spun around fast, glancing first at the horse, then in the direction it gazed. A bush some fifty yards away shook slightly, most people would have overlooked its movement as being caused by the wind. Not the Kid. He knew the bush moved without the aid of the wind.

"Look out, Mark!" he yelled, bringing up his rifle as he shouted the warning and firing as the last word left his mouth.

Three times the rifle crashed, its lever looking like a blur as he flipped it open and closed. Although the Kid spaced his shots along the bush, a spurt of flame licked out from it. An instant later, his third shot struck something. A rifle flew into the air from the bushes and he heard a startled yell.

Twisting around, the Kid looked to the edge of the ravine. Sick anxiety filled him, for the bullet had not been fired in his direction.

Two things saved Mark's life that day. The first was the Kid's shooting; which disturbed the would-be killer's aim. The second: his fast reflexes. On hearing the Kid's shout, Mark clamped a firm hold on the rope and dropped to his knees. Even so, the bullet grazed his shoulder and ripped his expensive shirt open. Pain caused him to loosen his hold and the rope shot through his fingers. Mark clamped his hands down on the rope,

then he remembered that stopping it dead might snap
the fibers. Gritting his teeth, he gradually slowed the
rope, feeling it burn his hands as it ran through.

Down below, Dusty thought his end had come. From
a steady, even glide, he dropped rapidly, then began to
slide faster. He heard the Kid's yell and the shots so
looked up, expecting to see Mark dropping with lead in
him. Then his fall slowed down, came to a gradual stop
for a couple of seconds. He hung on the end of the rope,
not looking down, fighting to regain control of his
racing pulse and startled nerves. Dusty was scared and
he did not give a damn who knew it. The difference between his fear and panic was that he held the fear in control and hung without trying to improve the situation.

Throwing a glance at Mark and seeing the big Texan
on his his knees but still holding the rope, the Kid turned
his attention to the would-be killer. He guessed his
bullet struck the rifle and batted it from its user's hands.
From what he could hear, rustling in the bushes, he
guessed the would-be killer was making for safety.

A low, deep-throated Comanche grunt left the Kid's
lips and he plunged into the bushes, leaping in pursuit of
the would-be killer. Whoever fired the shot proved to be
fleet of foot, for the Kid was no mean hand at running
and it took him some time to close the fifty-yard lead
the other had. At last he saw a moving splash of fawn
color among the greens and browns of the bushes. It
flickered in sight for an instant, then disappeared
behind a bush ahead of the Kid. Racing forward he
bounded the bush and crashed down on the buckskin
clad shape. They went to the ground, rolling over. The
Kid landed astride the would-be killer, kneeling and pin-
ning the writhing body to the ground. Up swung the
Kid's rifle, ready to drive the brass butt-plate into the
other's face.

"You!" he gasped, recognizing his captive through
the red mist of fury that had clouded his eyes, and

holding off his blow. Slowly, watchfully, he rose to his feet. "Get up and walk back there. If Dusty's fallen, you'll go in after him."

Dusty had not fallen, although it was touch and go for a few seconds. At last Mark gained full control of the rope and continued to lower Dusty at a slower, more even pace. Reaching below him, Dusty felt one of his feet touch a spike of rock. Gently Dusty felt his way around the rock and down on to firm ground.

"Are you all right, Dusty?" Mark called.

"Sure. Are you?"

"Somebody owes me a new shirt. Got a nick in my shoulder, there's nothing broke but it hurts like hell."

"Who did the shooting?"

"Damned if I know. Lon's took out after whoever it was."

Leaning against the ravine side, Dusty freed himself of his rope. Then he unfastened his bandana, shook loose its folds to fasten it over his nose and mouth. The stench of death hung in the air like a cloud and wearing his bandana over his face helped mask some of the vileness of the place. With that done, Dusty worked his way through the rocks towards where the body lay impaled.

Time ticked by. On top of the ravine, Mark put a hand up to feel at the wound on his shoulder. It appeared to be both wide and deep, but might have been far worse. Yet the wound would be dangerous for it bled freely and he still had to get Dusty out of the ravine. Taking out his handkerchief, Mark made a pad and held it to the wound. He was sweating and shaken. That had been a close call, the closest Mark could remember. Not only for himself, but for Dusty down below.

In the ravine, Dusty carried out his examination of the body, finding what he suspected. Picking up the revolver which lay at the side of the body, he thrust it into his waistband, then made his way to the wall and refastened the rope.

"Can you haul me up, Mark?" he called. "The sooner we're back to Casa Thackery the better."

"I reckon I can," Mark answered. "Make fast and yell out when you're ready."

"I'm ready now."

"You would be."

Mark drew in a deep breath and started to flex his muscles. The pad fell from his shoulder, but he let it lie. Now would be the most difficult part, raising Dusty's dead weight. They had never intended to fetch up the body, but Dusty would need to be brought out of the ravine as carefully as he went down into it. The question was, could Mark manage to haul his *amigo* up with that bad graze in his shoulder?

Gripping the rope, Mark hauled in the slack until he felt Dusty's weight at the other end.

"Take it easy, Mark!" Dusty yelled. "I'll get my feet against the wall and try to walk up. That should help."

"*Bueno!*" Mark answered. "This nick in my shoulder's a mite worse than I thought at first."

Although Mark tried to keep his anxiety from showing, Dusty heard and recognized it. If there had been less urgency in the situation, Dusty would have suggested waiting for the Kid's return before getting out of the ravine. What he had just seen told Dusty there was not a moment to lose, and that they must return to Casa Thackery with all speed.

Dusty leaned back against the rope and placed his right foot against the side of the ravine. He looked up at Mark who stood braced against the pull. Drawing in a deep breath, Dusty yelled, "Let's go!"

Taking the strain, Mark began to draw in on the rope. Down below, Dusty felt the pull and raised his other foot, stepping out and up. Slowly, placing each foot with care, Dusty started to walk up the sheer wall. In this manner he took some of the strain off Mark. However the blond giant still supported his weight and had to draw in on the rope.

In every way the climb out was more difficult than the lowering in. Going down, Dusty had been getting closer to the bottom and hanging feet down. If he had fallen then there would have been a slight chance that he might be able to avoid the rocks. On the way up, he rose higher with every step, leaning out at an angle from the wall. Should the rope break a knot slip, or Mark's strength fail, Dusty would fall backwards and have no chance of escaping being impaled on the rocks.

On top Mark stood breathing heavily, sweat poured down his face, into his eyes, and soaked his body. He felt the salty sting as sweat ran into his wound and wondered if sweat or blood soaked the back of his shirt. Both probably, he thought, clenching his teeth and continuing to haul in on the rope. The knots were hard to overcome. It meant taking one hand right away from the rope to grip over the joint and leaving Dusty's weight supported on the other. With Mark's good arm this did not greatly matter, but he had some bad moments when gripping the rope with his other hand and feeling the terrible pull on his injured shoulder.

Mark knew he did not dare hurry his pulling. A sudden jerk on the rope might cause Dusty to lose his footing and slip, and Mark knew his shoulder would not stand up to the weight of Dusty falling.

Just as Mark felt he could hold on no longer, but knew he must, he saw help coming. Shoving his prisoner ahead of him, the Kid came through the bushes. One glance told the Kid all he needed to know. Mark looked at the end of his tether and needed help about as bad as any man could want it. From the way the rope moved, Dusty must be alive at the other end of it. That fact alone saved the prisoner from instant death, for the Kid's forefinger trembled on the trigger of his rifle as he saw the blood on Mark's back.

"L-lend a hand, Lon!" Mark gasped.

The request for aid put the Kid in a hell of a spot. Already the prisoner had tried to kill Mark and bring about Dusty's death so would not hesitate to try again given half a chance. Such a chance would be offered while both Mark and the Kid had their hands full of rope. A sudden push might stagger them over the edge of the ravine, or cause them to loose the rope and drop Dusty to his death. Looking at Mark, the Kid knew there was not time to spare thinking of the prisoner's feelings. If Dusty was to be saved, the Kid must act quickly.

With a shove the Kid sent the prisoner sprawling to the ground just in front of his horse. Letting out an angry snort, the big white stallion stamped hard on the ground with a fore hoof and looked down with flaring nostrils and laid back ears at the human creature on the ground before it.

"Stay there!" order the Kid and added a warning as he turned towards Mark. "Ole Blackie'll stamp you flat if you move—and maybe if you don't."

Looking up at the seventeen-hand high white devil the Kid called Blackie, the prisoner did not doubt but what the black-dressed Texan spoke the simple truth.

Knowing the prisoner could give no further trouble, the Kid turned and ran to Mark's side. Laying his rifle down before them, the Kid reached for the rope.

"Easy!" Mark warned. "Dusty's walking up."

Watched by the hate-filled eyes of the prisoner, Mark and the Kid drew in on the rope. The worst danger had passed now. With the Kid's aid, Mark could manage to haul in the rope and bring Dusty to safety. For all that, Dusty's face showed some relief as it appeared at the edge of the ravine. Hooking a leg over the edge, Dusty held out a hand to the Kid and gratefully hauled himself on to solid ground.

"Thanks, Mark, Lon," he said, sitting on the ground by Mark as the big Texan sank to his knees.

"I had to save Lon's makings," Mark replied between gasps for breath. "I might get a smoke out of him before I bleed to death."

For once in his life the Kid did not challenge a remark about his smoking habits. Standing erect and looking off into the distance, the Kid gave silent thanks to *Ka-Dih* the Great Spirit of the Comanche. While not being a religious man, even to his grandfather's gods, the Kid reckoned he ought to give thanks to somebody that Mark and Dusty had come through that last fifteen minutes or so alive. They had been in tight spots before, but the Kid reckoned this had been the tightest and they could do without ever having to repeat it.

Just as Dusty turned to tell the Kid to fix Mark's shoulder, he saw the prisoner cowering before the menace of the white stallion. Although he was not particularly surprised at the prisoner's identity, the sight still gave him a bad shock.

"Jennie!" he gasped.

"She's the one who tried to shoot Mark," the Kid put in, moving towards his horse. "But I'm damned if I know why."

"I reckon I do," Dusty said quietly, his left hand rubbing the butt of the rusted old Navy Colt in his waistband. "Let her up, Lon, then tend to Mark."

Rising, Jennie came towards Dusty, her pale face working spasmodically as if she did not know whether to smile or cry at him. She halted a few feet away from him, stopped by the cold glow in his eyes. If Jennie had imagined her sex, or her grandfather's hopes, would sway Dusty her way, she now saw there was no hope of it happening.

"I—I didn't want to hurt you, Dustine," she said.

"Did you mean to hurt Marlene last night?" he answered.

For a guess, and it was no more, the words made a meat-in-the-pot hit. Cold anger glowed in the girl's eyes and an expression of hate twisted her face into something old and vicious, as mean as her grandfather always looked.

"Yes!" Jennie spat out. "I meant to hurt her. She ordered me to bed. *Me!* In Casa Thackery! She told me to go to bed as if she owned the house!''

Mark and the Kid peeked at the girl, then exchanged glances. They wondered how Jennie managed to get into the locked room, and what made Dusty suspect the girl.

''And you killed her,'' Dusty said quietly.

''I killed her,'' Jennie agreed. ''I went from my room and I watched her as she fought with Joan Shandley. It couldn't have worked better if I'd planned it. When Joan beat Aunt Marlene unconscious I saw my chance. I slipped up and hit Joan with the chair leg and then used the knife I brought on Aunt Marlene. The blood splashed my hand and dress but I didn't care. I knew how to take any suspicion from me.''

''Sure,'' Dusty drawled. ''Put Marlene's ring on Joan's finger, make sure everybody thought Joan killed Marlene and robbed her.''

''Yes. Then she would be tried for Aunt Marlene's murder and hanged for it.''

''Why Joan, Jennie?''

''She treated Grandfather like a saddle-tramp, humiliated him. I hated her. That was why we included her in the will. She was another one who wanted to take Casa Thackery from me, Dustine. They can't do it. I won't let them do it. Casa Thackery and everything Grandfather owns is mine. I had to fight for what belongs to me. Dustine, you must know how I feel.''

For a long moment Dusty did not reply. His eyes studied the girl's face as if he had never seen it before. Then an involuntary shudder ran through him.

''I don't know, Jennie,'' he said. ''And I hope to God I never do.''

CHAPTER ELEVEN

To Avenge Beegee Benson

Only a couple of Mexican house servants saw the three Texans bring Jennie back to Casa Thackery. The cow-hands, used to Borg's absence in a morning, went out to carry on with their work, and the people at the house stayed inside. Waco had been given certain orders by Dusty and the youngster obeyed them to the letter.

Leaving Jennie in the Kid's care, Dusty and Mark went to the house, using the kitchen. Dusty sent the cook to find the doctor and waited until Mark's wound received proper care before putting the next part of his plan into operation.

"You were lucky, Mark," the doctor stated. "That's a nasty gash up there."

"Yeah, I reckoned it might be, Doc," Mark replied. "And don't ask what happened, I hate lying."

"Got it cleaning your gun, huh?"

"You might say that," grinned Mark. "Fact being, until after Dusty gives the word I'd take it kind if you did say it."

"I'll go along with you," promised the doctor.

Dusty had been to see various people while Mark's wound received attention and he now returned carrying a new shirt for the blond giant, collected from his war-bag in the room.

"Let's go," he said. "Come with me, Doc. Mark, go tell Lon to bring her along like we planned."

171

Feeling puzzled, but interested, the doctor followed Dusty to the library. He found a good crowd gathered, which did not surprise Dusty who had arranged for them to be there. The sheriff sat scowling and wondering if he ought to have stood on his rights as senior law enforcement officer of the county and objected to Dusty ordering him to join the people in the room. Roughly the same thoughts ran through Claude Thackery's head; he wondered if he should have asked Dusty by what right he gave orders in Casa Thackery. Joan Shandley sat stiffly in a chair by Mamie Thackery, after the old woman and Frankie helped her downstairs. The local undertaker had come along because he possessed an inquisitive nature and wanted to know what went on in the grim old walls of the house.

Silence fell on the room and every eye went to Dusty as he walked from the door to halt before the crowd. He stood at the side of the room, looking across it, glancing at the fireplace and the portrait on the wall.

"Jennie's not in her room, Dustine," Mamie said. "I don't know where she is. Nobody's seen her all morning."

"She knows what I'm going to tell you," Dusty truthfully replied.

"What's it all about, Dusty?" Gaunt asked.

"Sheriff," Dusty said, ignoring the question. "You never checked on that body in the ravine, did you?"

"Shucks, everybody could see it was Elmo," Topham replied.

"He the only white-haired old man around here?"

"Naw. Course he ain't, Cap'n. There's old Bill Turner——"

"Ain't seen old Bill around for some weeks now," the doctor interrupted Topham to announce. "Been by his place three times and he wasn't there."

"Hell, Doc!" snorted Topham. "You know old Bill takes off prospecting every once in a while. Anyways, that couldn't've been Bill. Them two cowhands who found the body said it was wearing the same clothes they'd seen Elmo in not an hour afore they found him.''

"What're your questions leading to, Dusty?" Gaunt put in.

"That feller in the ravine," Dusty answered. "He was shot in the back before he went over."

The words created something of a sensation. Talk welled up among the occupants of the room and was silenced by an angry gesture from Topham who came to his feet.

"Now just a doggoned minute. I been out there and looked down into the ravine. Me 'n' my deputies. We couldn't see no sign of a bullet wound. And them two cowhands who found Elmo who close enough to have heard a shot."

"But you never went into the ravine and looked real close, did you, sheriff?" asked Dusty.

"Naw. Hell, you seen that place. What with it being an accident, and that bit about leaving him lie if he died someplace like that ravine, and all, we didn't see the sense of risking men's lives to go down there. Elmo was for sure dead and it wouldn't fetch him back to life if somebody else got killed too. So we got the preacher to say words over him and left him where he fell."

"And a killer was left to do more killing," Dusty snapped. "Three people have died, and another one nearly got killed, all because you didn't check."

"I assume some of the responsibility for that, Dusty," Gaunt remarked.

"If it comes to that, I said we should give Elmo his dying request," Mamie went on. "Three—— You said three people died. Is Jennie——"

"I didn't count her," Dusty answered, choosing his words carefully. "We, Mark, Lon and I, went out there today. While Mark was lowering me into the ravine, somebody took a shot at us."

"Who?" Gaunt asked, wondering why Dusty spoke much louder than usual and put extra clarity into his words as if he wanted them to carry some distance.

"Jennie."

"Jennie!" At least four voices repeated the word Dusty spoke.

"Is she dead?" gasped Mamie.

"When the Kid heard the shot, he turned, saw a movement in the bushes and started throwing lead—from his rifle."

The last three words gave a special significance to the listeners, for all knew of the Kid's amazing skill with a rifle. Once more silence dropped on the room and Dusty waited to see if the bait would draw the killer into his trap. For almost thirty seconds nothing happened.

"Is she d——" Thackery finally said.

Even as the lawyer spoke, a sound drew every eye to the fireplace. Its back swung open and, as Dusty hoped would happen, the killer of Casa Thackery burst into the room—but Dusty's plan only partially worked.

"Elmo!" Mamie screamed and collapsed back in her chair looking as if she was seeing a ghost.

"Father!" Claude screeched, looking as if he had seen something worse than a ghost; such as the ownership of Casa Thackery departing from his grasp.

Dusty did not speak or move. The old Walker Colt in Elmo Thackery's right hand lined full on Frankie's breast and the shotgun gripped on the old man's claw-like left hand pointed down to the floor.

"Sit still, all of you!" he snarled. "The gal gets it if you move."

While Dusty expected Thackery to be listening to the meeting and to make his appearance on hearing of Jennie's "death," the small Texan had also expected the man to be so shocked at the news that he would not be able to think straight. The gun in Thackery's hand showed that Dusty had guessed only partly right.

"Who is that in the ravine, if you're alive!" Gaunt asked.

"Old Bill Turner," Thackery answered. "Doing

something useful for once in his life. Where's the Kid. Did he kill my Jennie?''

"Look at the door," Dusty, to whom the words had been directed, replied.

Jennie came in, the Kid's hand on her arm. On seeing her grandfather, the girl jerked herself free and ran to his side. She did not pass before him or in any way interfere with his keeping Frankie covered.

"Get the scatter, little gal!" Thackery ordered. "Stand easy all of you."

"Drop the gun and give it up, Elmo," Dusty ordered. "You'll never get away from here."

"Maybe we don't aim to," Thackery replied. "Call Mark Counter in here."

"He's in the hall, Grandfather!" Jennie put in, holding the shotgun with easy familiarity.

"Call him in, Dustine!" Thackery said and gestured towards Frankie. "And he best come empty handed."

"Come in with your hands empty, Mark!" Dusty called.

Holstering his right side Colt, Mark entered the library, his hands held clear of the gun butts. He looked around him, to where Waco stood at the far side of the room, the Kid at the left of the door, Dusty standing before the people who all stared in amazement and horror at Jennie and Elmo Thackery.

"I don't reckon he'd kill Frankie," Mark said quietly.

"Don't try him," Dusty answered. "He tried last night, with the rattler."

"It'd've worked too," Thackery spat out. "It did when I tried it out afore on that greaser gal servant."

"You did better on Borg," Dusty admitted. "Only it didn't look like suicide, Elmo. You should have held the gun to one side, instead of right behind his head."

"Yeah," grunted Thackery. I should have. Only he sat up on the bed just after I come out of the cupboard with his gun in his hand and I couldn't risk him turning and seeing me. So I shot him and he fell forward off the bed. I thought it'd only be Topham there investigating and he'd fall for it. Should have knowed you'd butt in, Dustine. You're nosey, just like your Uncle Devil.''

"What do we do about them, Grandfather?" Jennie asked.

"Nothing yet. How long you known about me, Dustine, and who've you told?"

"I've not told anybody. But I suspected you when I saw the rattler," Dusty answered, watching for a chance to break the deadlock without getting Frankie hurt. "That's when I started thinking about you being alive, Elmo. I was suspicious as soon as I heard about the hit at Joan in Newton. That attack on us in the Nations made more sure. Knowing you, there wouldn't be many saw your will. I didn't even think Aunt Mamie had. So it left Frank, and I trusted him, and Jennie. She was sure to know about your will. Why ask Uncle Devil to have us gather the folks?"

"To show folks how keen I was to get them here. Sending the famous Dusty Fog, Mark Counter and the Ysabel Kid after them. Only it'd be just too bad happen they all got killed when a bunch of raiders hit Dusty Fog's camp to try to steal his trail drive money. I reckon I handled it real well."

"You overdid it, like everything else," Dusty drawled. "There was too much happened just right. Like your death coming just when we'd be either in or real close to Mulrooney. You'd seen our trail herd passing north——"

"Sure I had. I'd planned all this earlier though. Couldn't've worked out better, you making for the railroad and all them four being within easy reach."

"I still say you overdid it. That piece in your will about leaving your body lie where it fall, it didn't have any real point unless the body went into a place where folks'd think twice about trying to recover it. You knew Mamie and Frank would respect your last wishes, and that Topham wasn't going to push it too hard at inspecting the body when he saw the risks involved. So nobody'd know it wasn't Elmo Thackery lying out there.''

"That's right," Thackery answered, his eyes gloating at the thought of his brilliant plan. He could not prevent himself boasting, telling everything. "Turner came to see me. I sent for him, the night afore and Jennie dropped him. We dressed him in my clothes, some like I was wearing when those cowhands saw me, and took him out to the ravine, tossed him over. Next day I rode up there, turned my hoss loose after I made him rear at the edge, and hid out in the bushes. Come back here and got hid in the priest's hole behind the fireplace that night. There's secret passages all round this house, only me 'n' Jennie knowed 'em.''

"I guessed about them, even though Jennie lied about there being any," Dusty told the old man, hoping the gun would waver, but it did not. "You used the one that came out in the cupboard in our room when you went to put the snake in Frankie's bed. That's why Jennie was so all-fired eager to keep us downstairs. I nearly caught you at it, didn't I?''

"And I saved your life, Dustine," Jennie put in. "What do we do about them, Grandfather?''

"I know why you wanted Claude and Marlene dead," Dusty put in, before the old man could reply. "You was scared they'd contest your will and take some of the land or money from Jennie. And you aimed to get rid of the only other two, Mamie and Frankie, who had any legal claim. But why Borg?''

He got drunk one night. Told me it was his father who put me where I am today. That he ought to marry Jennie so that he could get hands on my money. I should have killed him then. But I didn't. I let him live long enough to think he had a share in my money. Than I killed him.''

"Why me?" Joan asked.

"You?" Jennie spat out. "You thought my Grand-father was an old bag-line bum and you bought him a meal as if he was a tramp. That's why."

"I didn't want you to get here," Thackery went on. "So I fixed it with a feller. I know to have a pair of gun-nies follow you when he heard about my death, and not to kill you until you knew about the money I'd left you. I wanted you to know it wasn't a bag-line bum you'd helped. Last night, I thought you and Marlene was going to kill each other. But you didn't, Jennie here fixed it neat so you'd be blamed after she killed Marlene."

"You killed her!" Claude screamed and started to rise.

The shotgun in Jennie's hand boomed, its charge slamming into Claude's chest and hurling him back across the room, smashing the chair beneath him. Frankie screamed, but kept her seat; nor did the Walker Colt's muzzle waver from line on the girl's body, so Dusty did not have a chance to make a move.

"He won't take Casa Thackery from us now, Grand-father," Jennie said, her lips twisting into a mirthless smile that went well with the mad gleam in her eyes.

"Keep still, all of you!" Thackery warned. "And I reckon you boys had best shed your gunbelts."

Slowly Joan Shandley moved her right hand into the mouth of the vanity bag she had carried with her all morning and which now rested on her knees. Inside it lay a Remington Double Derringer, an item most saloongirls carried on their persons when working in wild wide-open towns. She had packed the Derringer with her other belongings when she left Newton, never expecting to need it. The incidents since her arrival at Casa Thackery had caused her to unpack the gun again and hide it in the bag. Now it seemed she might have use for the gun.

Looking towards Dusty, Joan saw the indecison on his face. He, and every man in the room, knew that the moment they dropped their guns they would be dead men. Thackery and his granddaughter were crazy enough to try to kill every person in the room.

"You sent men to kill me?" Joan asked and saw Thackery's mean, evilly glinting eyes turn towards her.

"Had it done. Same feller as fixed with them raiders to hit at you done it for me," Thackery replied. "And I ain't askin'——"

"Beegee Benson died, not me!" Joan said bitterly.

Flame spurted from the bag. Joan was a poor shot, never having practised with the gun. So her bullet missed Thackery—and struck Jennie in the left breast. The impact spun Jennie around and pain caused her to squeeze the shotgun's second trigger. Its lethal charge smashed into the wall within inches of the Ysabel Kid's side. *Ka-Dih* appeared to be watching over Long Walker's grandson that day.

On the shot Thackery's head jerked around and the Walker's barrel sagged down out of line. Half a second later he was dead.

Seven hands moved the instant the gun no longer lined on Frankie's body. Seven hands trained in the lightning fast withdrawal of weapons and skilled in aiming the weapons when they lifted clear of leather.

Ahead of the others, Dusty's matched Colts roared, their lead ripping into Thackery's head and shattering it like a pumpkin tossed against a wall. Mark's ivory butted Peacemakers bellowed an instant behind Dusty's and about the same amount ahead of Waco's Army Colts making their music. A good quarter of a second later, last of the quartet into action, the Ysabel Kid's old Dragoon vomited a .44 ball in a thunder-clap roar and a spurt of flame.

Elmo Thackery might not have died out there by the ravine, but he sure as hell was dead when his body smashed into the wall by the fireplace, hung there for a moment, then pitched forward on to his face. There were seven bullets in his body; four of .45 caliber, three a mere .44 in size. Any one of them would have killed him.

Powder-smoke whirled and eddied around the room. Frankie screamed again and twisted herself into her aunt's arms, shutting her eyes to hide the sight she had just witnessed. The men stayed still as statues for a moment, then the girl's sobbing jolted Dusty into action.

"Frank, get the women out of here!" he snapped. "Doc, look to Jennie."

Holstering his guns, Waco sprang forward. With surprising gentleness he drew the almost hysterical little girl from Mamie's arms and carried her from the room. Gaunt knocked the vanity bag from Joan's hand and stamped on it, for the exploding powder's flames had set fire to the material. With the fire out, he ushered Mamie and Joan out of the room.

Kneeling by Jennie, the doctor looked up to Dusty and shook his head. One glance had told him already that the two male Thackerys had passed beyond any human aid.

"If I had some of the new gear they've brought out in the East I might be able to do something, Dusty," he said. "But there's no chance for her with what I have here."

"Maybe it's all for the best, Doc," Dusty replied.

Crossing the room without a glance at the bodies, the Kid entered the open priest-hole and looked around. He had seen such rooms in Mexican *haciendas* and knew what to expect. The room was small, square shaped, with a second entrance opening on to one of the passages built within the walls by some long forgotten architect. A small table stood to the right of the fireplace door, a solitary chair by it. Across the room was a small, thin bed, not much comfort for a man as rich as Elmo Thackery had been. The Kid's eyes went to the block of stone on the table. It had been pulled out of the wall over a stout stone shelf above the fireplace door. Climbing on to the table, the Kid used it as a step to mount the shelf. He would be behind the portrait; a pair of holes, most likely in the eyes of one of the figures, allowed him to see what went on in the library and hear what the men in the room said with surprising clarity.

A man had to hand it to Dusty, way he figured this whole stinking mess out. Dusty had guessed that Thackery was hidden in the house and would be on hand to spy on any meeting held in the library. Playing on Thackery's love for Jennie, Dusty hinted that she had been killed in an attempt to bring the man out of hiding. That was the reason for Dusty speaking louder than usual, the Kid could now tell he did not need to have troubled, an ordinary voice, by some trick of acoustics, could be clearly heard from the look-out place behind the portrait.

"So this's where he hid out, huh?" Topham's voice said from below. "Hey, where you at, Kid?"

"Up here," the Kid replied and the startled man jerked back to crack his head on the low door. "This's how somebody managed to kill Marlene Thackery and get out of a room leaving the door and windows locked on the inside. It sure as hell spoiled your open and shut case."

"Huh!" grunted Topham. "I never really thought Miss Shandley'd done it."

Miss Shandley would now be a third owner in the Thackery fortune and it did not pay to speak disrespectfully of powerful folks in the county, so Topham was hoping his words would reach Joan's ears and cancel out any anger she might feel at his earlier suspicions.

Jumping down, The Kid looked around the small room. "Lordy Lord. Elmo sure must have hated folks to live down here ever since he was supposed to have died."

"Miss Jennie must've brought him food," Topham answered. "And he likely got out in the fresh air at nights."

"Just like you say," drawled the Kid and walked out of the room with Topham hot on his heels.

"Cap'n Fog and Mark went outside," the undertaker told the Kid.

Despite his profession, the undertaker looked a mite green around the gills. He did not get much trade in his sideline—he actually ran the general store for a living—and did not care to have it delivered wholesale like this.

Mark found Dusty standing on the porch, leaning on the stone rail and looking across the range. For a moment neither man spoke, then Dusty seemed to become aware of his big *amigo* at his side.

"How's the shoulder, Mark?" he asked.

"Still there," Mark replied. "How are *you*?"

"Sick to my guts. I knew that girl when she was as sweet, fresh and likeable as Frankie. That was how Jennie was first time I saw her. But she changed. Lord, how she changed. I saw the change when Elmo brought her down to Polveroso and tried to marry us off. He warped Jennie the way he was warped, turned her as mean and miserly as himself. I never regretted killing a man less, Mark."

"Do you want me to get the boys and saddle the horses?"

"No. I'll pull through. And we'll have to help the women over this lot."

At that moment the Kid came from the house, like Mark, he guessed at Dusty's mood. Walking forward, he sat on the stone rail and sucked in a breath of fresh air. It seemed unusually good after the acrid stink of burnt powder mingled with human blood and the musty, decayed stench of the priest's hole.

"How'd you reckon Elmo allowed to come back after they'd got rid of all the legatees, Dusty?" he asked.

"We'll never know. Maybe he figured to appear one day and allow he'd been hit over the head and couldn't remember who he was. He might even have thought he could just come back and nobody's dare think anything wrong."

"He'd be plumb loco if he thought that," Mark stated.

"Nothing he did was the act of a sane man," Dusty replied. "This whole affair, the way he planned every move of it, no sane man would have done all that. He was obsessed with the idea that everything he owned went to Jennie, and he turned her the same way. So they tried to make sure nobody ever laid hands on a cent of it. Lord, I wish Uncle Devil had never straddled us with this chore."

"Look at it this way, same as me and Lon do, Dusty," Mark answered. "Happen we hadn't been along, Aunt Mamie, Frankie and Joan would be dead now, or real soon."

"That's the only consolation to it," Dusty said. "Let's go back inside."

Casa Thackery did not die. It took much long persuasion on Dusty's part to prevent the spread going by the board. At first none of the three women wanted anything to do with the house, for it held too many evil associations and memories. At last Dusty showed them how many people depended on the Thackery ranch for a living and they agreed to have the place run by a manager.

The shock of all she had seen made Frankie ill. Mamie and Joan left their affairs in Gaunt's hand while they took the girl East. They were to travel almost around the world before she recovered and would never set foot in Texas again.

Three days after Elmo Thackery's second, and final, death, the two women left for the east with Frankie. On the same day Dusty Fog, Mark Counter, the Ysabel Kid and Waco rode south, headed for the Rio Hondo country.

"I sure hope lil Short-Stop gets well," Waco told the others as they passed over a rim and out of sight of Casa Thackery.

"It's maybe a good thing she's going east," replied Mark with a grin.

"Leave him be, Mark," Dusty ordered. "Haven't you ever been in love?"

"Not if I could avoid it," answered Mark, then he remembered something the Kid had said in Mulrooney before they took on Thackery's chore. "Lon, the next time you allow we're going to have an easy time on something, keep quiet about it. You're just tempting old *Ka-Dih* to make things awkward for us."

J.D. HARDIN

**"THE MOST EXCITING
WESTERN WRITER SINCE
LOUIS L'AMOUR"
—JAKE LOGAN**

___ 872-16840-9	BLOOD, SWEAT AND GOLD	$1.95
___ 872-16842-5	BLOODY SANDS	$1.95
___ 867-21039-7	SONS AND SINNERS	$1.95
___ 872-16869-7	THE SPIRIT AND THE FLESH	$1.95
___ 867-21226-8	BOBBIES, BAUBLES AND BLOOD	$2.25
___ 06572-3	DEATH LODE	$2.25
___ 06138-8	HELLFIRE HIDEAWAY	$2.25
___ 06380-1	THE FIREBRANDS	$2.25
___ 06410-7	DOWNRIVER TO HELL	$2.25
___ 06001-2	BIBLES, BULLETS AND BRIDES	$2.25
___ 06331-3	BLOODY TIME IN BLACKTOWER	$2.25
___ 06248-1	HANGMAN'S NOOSE	$2.25
___ 06337-2	THE MAN WITH NO FACE	$2.25
___ 06151-5	SASKATCHEWAN RISING	$2.25
___ 06412-3	BOUNTY HUNTER	$2.50
___ 06743-2	QUEENS OVER DEUCES	$2.50
___ 07017-4	LEAD LINED COFFINS	$2.50
___ 06845-5	SATAN'S BARGAIN	$2.50
___ 06850-1	THE WYOMING SPECIAL	$2.50
___ 07259-2	THE PECOS DOLLARS	$2.50
___ 07257-6	SAN JUAN SHOOTOUT	$2.50
___ 07379-3	OUTLAW TRAIL	$2.50
___ 07392-0	THE OZARK OUTLAWS	$2.50
___ 07461-7	TOMBSTONE IN DEADWOOD	$2.50
___ 07381-5	HOMESTEADER'S REVENGE	$2.50

Prices may be slightly higher in Canada.